OUT OF BODY

Suzanne Brockmann

Suzanne Brockmann Books
www.SuzanneBrockmann.com

www.SuzanneBrockmann.com
Email Newsletter: *News from Suz*: https://tinyletter.com/SuzanneBrockmann
www.BookBub.com/authors/suzanne-brockmann
www.Twitter.com/SuzBrockmann
www.Facebook.com/SuzanneBrockmannBooks

For Jason T. Gaffney and Kevin Held, the actors for whom the screenplay of *Out of Body* was written.

I know they'd want me to say this loudly: FOR THE LOVE OF LOVE, register, double-check that you remain registered, and #VoteBLUE !!

Out of Body is soon to be an indie feature rom-com movie, starring Jason T. Gaffney and Kevin Held, filming in California in September 2018. Support LGBTQ cinema and help us Kickstart it! Find out more at www.SuzanneBrockmann.com/movies

CHAPTER ONE
Henry

It's Halloween, it's Halloween...

Back when I was around ten years old, I made the brutal mistake of being in the room when my mother played a song about Halloween by a "band" called the Shaggs, and from that moment, after just one listen, it became a permanent ear-worm for my favorite holiday.

Google it if you dare. I recommend you don't. You'll never un-hear it.

Still, I was okay with that—it made me smile. And it became part of my yearly tradition. I would decorate my house with the song (Can it really be called a song? More like a collection of sounds and words...) playing in my head—*Why, even Dracula will be there!*

This year, after I did my morning workout and tended my garden, I had my good friend Gina's voice in my ear, too. Because she called me in the middle of it all. And you can't not-answer when Gina calls.

"Tonight's the night," she proclaimed. Gina doesn't ease into conversations with mundane greetings or pleasantries like, *Hello, Henry. It's Gina. How are you?*

I purposely pretended to misunderstand. "It is!" I said cheerfully. "The night of the big party!"

"No, it's the night your ridiculous bromance with Malcolm turns into the *romance* it should've been from the start," she sternly corrected me. "It's the night you finally seize the day."

My long-time friend, Mal—best friend, really—was a novelist whose day job was to copy-edit other writers' books. He would've leapt all over Gina's statement: the *night* you seize the *day*...? I'm a photographer, however, and I got the picture.

"Or you could just continue doing and saying nothing," she added, "pathetically waiting for some impossibly perfect moment, which will never come. If you wait *too* long he'll hook up with another loser like Don or Jeff and you'll have to best-friend him through *that* nightmare—God forbid he *marries* the man…"

"No, you're right," I told her. Told myself, too. She *was* right. "If not now, then when. I get it, Gina, I do." I attempted to pep-talk myself. "And Halloween would make a great anniversary, considering how much Mal likes my candy-corn cake…" Wow, that sounded way stupider when I said it aloud.

But Gina didn't mock me. "It's perfect timing," she agreed.

But how was I gonna do this—this magical friends-to-lovers transformation…? "We've been friends for years. What am I supposed to do? Just grab him and kiss him?"

"Yes!" she shouted so loudly I had to pull the phone from my ear. "Brilliant! That'll be my cue to make everyone leave."

"Yeah, no," I told her. Even if I lost my mind and decided to take Gina's act-first-talk-later approach, I wasn't gonna do it in front of an audience. "God, I'm regretting telling you…" *If* I lost my mind…? I had to laugh. Apparently, I'd already lost it when I'd idiotically blurted to Gina that I'd been thinking about Mal in a much more than friends-ish way. Still, maybe it was similar to telling a friend that you were going to eat healthier. It applied the pressure needed to make you skip the fried food and have the turkey burger. Saying it aloud made you go for the goal…

I thought about my goal—about Mal, in my life as a boyfriend, a partner, a *lover*… God, I wanted that, more than I could put into words.

Gina was pretty good at reading my mind. "It's gonna be okay," she promised. "Whatever happens. But really, Henry, you *have* to try. Don't chicken out."

I couldn't promise that I wouldn't. "See you tonight," I told her instead.

"I'm bringing my Ouija board," she announced. "Oh! And Carl."

The Ouija board, I'd expected. It had been a constant in our Halloween celebrations since Gina had found it at a garage sale when we were in seventh grade. But before I could say *Wait, do you mean Carl-from-college-who-moved-to-London Carl or some new Carl…?*, she'd already hung up. It couldn't be a boyfriend—Gina was happily married. Her husband was in the Navy and serving overseas.

I thought about calling her back for about zero-point-two seconds, but opted instead for waiting and finding out the answer to the Carl mystery tonight. In the meantime, I had a cake to bake, and a closet to sift through, in search of the perfect shirt to wear on the grand occasion of finally grabbing and kissing my old friend Mal.

Malcolm

I was running late.

Really late.

Like, inexcusably, unforgivably late.

Which, if I were, say, a paramedic or an ER doctor, would've been instantly forgiven.

"Yeah, hey, Henry, sorry I'm late to your Halloween party. Had to save a life. Up to my elbows again in aortas and clamps. You know how it goes…"

But no. I was late to my best friend's favorite holiday event because the author whose book I was copy-editing hadn't gotten his revisions in on time.

My deadline didn't move. Which meant I had to do a week of work in seventeen hours. And miss most of Henry's party.

By the time I arrived, nearly everyone had already gone home.

Because of that, I was able to park on the street right in front of Henry's little house in his crowded Sherman Oaks neighborhood. As I started up the path, I saw that the world's oldest trick-or-treater— dressed as a harried, exhausted father—had just rung the doorbell on Henry's festively decorated front stoop.

Despite the fact that it was closing in on midnight and well past the proper trick-or-treating hour, Henry answered the door with a big smile and his equally giant bowl of candy.

God, Henry loved Halloween.

He definitely knew the man who was standing there. I wasn't close enough to hear what they said as they conversed, but I didn't need to. Henry's expressive face went from welcoming smile, to surprise, to concern, and then into a full-blown, triumphant *eureka!*

I'd seen that exact look on H's face many times in our decade-plus of friendship. He had an idea, and believe-you-me, it was gonna be *great*.

I couldn't help but smile myself as I stood there watching, in the middle of Henry's beautifully tended front garden, as he said something that turned his harried-parent trick-or-treater into grateful-and-far-more-relaxed still-hot-dad. And then I had to laugh as Henry pulled the man's jack-o'-lantern patterned trick-or-treat bag closer and dumped his entire giant bowl of candy into the damn thing.

Grateful Dad laughed and then grabbed Henry and hugged him hard. I knew what that felt like—as gay men, H and I were both rampant huggers, and over the past dozen years, we'd hugged a time or two-thousand. Henry was nearly as tall as me, but he was lithe. Slender. Willowy. With an ass that... Well. With a dancer's ass. He'd danced in high school and he still worked out daily. He ran for miles—kill me now. And he did some weird cross-fit shit that he combined with his relentless gardening, that was oddly riveting—to watch, that is.

Back in college, I'd been inappropriately into him. Inappropriate, because I was his senior dorm RA, and he was this adorable, literally *fresh*person who pretty much deified me. Through that very first year of our friendship, I learned to disconnect—basically go out of body—whenever Henry enthusiastically hugged me. Why? Because I was—and let's face it, I *still* am—a mess, and he didn't yet know that he deserved far better. And no way was I gonna take advantage of his giant-blue-anime-eyed hero-worship.

Somehow—I still don't know how—I managed to *not* fuck up our friendship.

I managed to *not* take advantage of one of those hundreds of impetuous Henry-hugs, and I managed to *always* let him go when he pulled back. (Yes, I'm splitting infinitives—AKA the Star Trek exception—for emphasis, because back when we first met, I definitely would've been boldly going *et cetera*. He was *that* much of a sweet young thing.) Time after time, I managed to *not* turn his friendly embrace into something more and kiss him—even though I know he would've welcomed my tongue in his mouth.

I managed to *not* fuck him sideways, into Tuesday. Or Wednesday. Or, let's face it, halfway into next month.

I'm kinda good at fucking.

But I kinda suck at every part of a romantic relationship that's *not* fucking.

So I was standing there, watching Hot Formerly-Harried Dad hugging my pal Henry, and every cell in my body suddenly clenched. Like, *Fuck, I wanna be inside him...*

Of course, *that* was when Henry spotted me.

Standing there, lustfully gaping at him like a lustful, gaping idiot.

"Hey, Mal, you made it!" Henry said gaily (pun intended), even as he gently extracted himself from his hugger's grip. "Tell Joey to feel better," he told the man.

"Thanks again, Henry," Joey's dad said, smiling vaguely in my obviously far less-attractive direction as he hoofed it toward the street.

Henry greeted me, of course, with a hug. He tugged me inside his house, set his now-empty bowl on the table in his entry, closed and locked the door, then turned off the lights.

"Wow, I made it just in time," I said. "Pull up the drawbridge, too, why don't you?"

"Halloween is over," Henry agreed. "I'm kinda outa candy."

"Because you gave it all to..." I left a generous pause that said *Please fill in the name of the man who was just hugging the shit out of you.* But then I remembered what I'd heard him say. "...the dad of... Joey... who doesn't feel well?"

"Joey has a stomach bug," Henry told me.

"Oh! So his dad is trick or treating *for* him, and you just saved Dad's ass by giving him all your candy." It was after eleven, and Joey's dad no doubt would not be greeted as cheerfully by their other neighbors. And, since Henry insisted on a Halloween bowl that was eclectic and diverse—a fine mix of chocolate and fruit-flavored candies—Joey's dad's job was done. Aside from, you know, sitting up with the kid and cleaning up the puke. "Suddenly, it makes sense."

"Joey's only four—he's adorable," Henry told me, his giant heart in his big blue eyes. Talk about adorable... "And he's missing Halloween."

"That's almost as tragic as being thirty-four and having to work late. But, I finally finished the copy edit from hell."

"You did?" Henry was excited at my news. I'd been texting him my pain throughout much of the ordeal. Of course, he regularly and good-naturedly absorbed my rants and lectures about the vital need for Oxford commas, the fact that *a lot* is two goddamn words, and it's *fewer*, people, as in *Ten Items or Fewer*, for the love of leaping Jesus. "Thank God!"

"I did, thank *all* the gods," I agreed. "The gruesome serial killer book is off my desk. Your Halloween might officially be over, but mine is just starting. So. Who's still here and what'd I miss?"

CHAPTER TWO
Still Malcolm

After filling me in on the night's drama, Henry led me into the living room where Gina jumped out of her seat.

"Hey, you," she said. "About time you got here!"

She'd been sitting at H's funky bar-height table, where her glorious and clearly hand-made Ouija board had been set up. And speaking of glorious, a very nice looking, very jacked, very obviously gay man of color was still sitting at that table, eyebrows slightly raised as he watched Gina hug me. The two of them were all that remained of Henry's Halloween extravaganza—everyone else had already gone home. It was, after all, a work night.

"Henry says the Ouija board just spelled *cake*," I said. "And… you brought him an actual *orb* from the *spirit world*…?"

"And Carl," Henry added. "Gina also brought Carl. Carl, Malcolm; Mal, Carl."

Carl—the man still sitting at the table—held out his hand, so I shook it. Strong, sure grip. I liked him instantly. But then, maybe I didn't. Had Gina brought this extremely attractive man for Henry…?

"Carl just moved to LA from New York," Gina informed me. She was petite and Asian American and effortlessly pretty, with a warm smile and deep brown eyes. She'd been friends with Henry for even more years than I had—since third grade, I think. So that meant that in the ongoing Who's Henry's Best-Friend Contest that was Gina v. Mal (i.e. every time we occupied the same real estate), she won. Always. And she made sure I knew it. But she loved Henry fiercely, so I was okay with that. "I couldn't leave him alone on Halloween."

"Yeah, you really could've," Carl said.

Gina wrapped her arms around his massive shoulders in a hug on her way back to her seat. "No, I could not've. Besides, we need an even number for the Ouija board to work."

"Yeeeeah," Carl said, drawing the word out this time, "I'm gonna hafta object to a sentence that includes both *Ouija board* and *work.*"

"Carl's a skeptic." Henry's warm smile wasn't just for me, it was also for Carl, and my entire world stuttered in a weird panic, God help me. Which was stupid, since it had been far too many months since Henry had broken up with his last boyfriend—a tragic twink-shaped mistake named Brian who was a lying little shit of a cheater.

I took a deep breath, and forced my face into a smile. This was a party. We were having fun! Yay! And the truth was, I desperately wanted Henry to be happy. And if Carl entered our lives already thoroughly vetted by Gina, that was a *good* thing. Right?

Right.

I managed to ungrit my teeth as I choked out a noise that was vaguely laughter-like. "Okay. Help me out here, people. What's not working about a Ouija Board that spells *cake?*"

Henry laughed, and gestured toward the side table where—oh my God, I actually gasped aloud—a full half of his traditional Halloween cake, with its orange and black frosting, had survived the hungry hoard.

I couldn't help myself as I helped myself, knowing that Henry had probably stood nearby and said *Let's make sure we save a piece for Malcolm* to every one of his guests. "Thank you Henry and baby Jesus! I was sure I'd missed your epic candy corn cake."

Henry was health-conscious, as always. "Did you skip dinner?" he asked me. "I saved you a plate."

"Oh, thanks," I said through a mouthful of sugar-filled deliciousness, "but I grabbed a sandwich a few hours ago." I turned back to the table with the Ouija board. And the too-attractive man still sitting there. Attractively. Henry's future husband. I thought it might help if I mentally called him that, but nope. "So. Carl. Do you work with Gina…?"

Henry answered for him. "Yeah, but they were also roommates at NYU."

"Ah!" This was *that* Carl. "Henry and I met back in college, too," I said, as I sat down across from Gina.

Carl nodded. "That's impressive. You two've been together for, what, twelve years?"

What…? Together…? I laughed wildly as I looked over at Henry to share the absurd joke that we might actually be a couple, but his back was to me—he'd begun organizing the leftover food.

"Oh God, no, we're not together, like *together*," I said, my voice sounding a bit too loudly jocular, even to my own ears. "I mean, we're *friends*, yeah... For..." I mentally did the math. "...*more* than twelve years. Wow. That *is* a long time."

"It *is*," Gina agreed, then told Carl, "They have the most amazing meet-cute. Malcolm was the RA in Henry's freshman dorm."

Henry did glance up at that. "Meet-cute. Are you kidding?" He told Carl, "We met in the bathroom after my first-ever college party. I was throwing up." He winced as he met my eyes. "I'm still so sorry."

I held up my plate. "You've long since paid me back."

"It's the fact that Mal stayed in there with you, all night long," Gina told Henry, "that makes it so damn cute."

"Just doin' my job, ma'am," I said, pretending that I'd pulled similar all-nighters with the other freshmen on our floor, when in truth I had not.

Gina huffed at me, which was generally a sign that I was doing something wrong, so I checked to make sure I wasn't wearing chocolate frosting as an accidental Halloween accessory, but nope. Nothing on my shirt. Still, she was giving me her stank eye.

I'm pretty sure I hadn't farted, so...

Ohhh... Shit, maybe I'd messed up Gina's carefully-planned romantic evening for Henry and Carl by getting here so late. Oops, and I'd planned to ask H if I could crash on his sofa tonight—I had an early morning meeting in Studio City. A potential new client—I could not be late. *That* was going to be awkward, asking to stay over, but... no. Nah. Come on. I mentally slapped myself upside the head. Henry wasn't going to have a romantic evening of the sleepover variety with a guy that he barely knew, and Gina knew it. We all did, except maybe Carl, who was going to have to *earn* the precious gift that was Henry's love, goddamn it. He couldn't just show up and help himself like he was at some $9.99 buffet...

So now I was sitting there, eating my cake and giving a far more subtle stink eye to Carl, when Gina pointedly and deliberately changed the subject. "Oh, hey, Henry, I'd been meaning to ask you. Any recent sightings of Hot Neighbor Guy?"

What...? I'm pretty sure my head snapped up at that. Who...?

Henry cleared his throat. "I may have seen him again this morning."

Okay, so he wasn't talking about Hot-Dad-of-Joey, who he'd seen just minutes ago... Now *I* cleared my throat. "Um, I don't believe I've heard about Hot Neighbor Guy."

Gina was grinning at me in gleeful delight, and when she first started to speak, I got confused, thinking she was talking to me. "You gonna make a move on him? Kiss him passionately?"

But no, she was asking this of Henry, in reference to this so-called Hot Neighbor Guy. She finally turned toward him as she kept going. "Throw him to the ground? Fuck his brains out...?"

Henry was "cleaning up" a nearly empty bowl of candy corn by polishing off the remains, and he nearly choked.

"*That* escalated rapidly," I said, ready to leap to my feet to Heimlich him if he needed it.

But he didn't—he was able to speak. "He's just... a new neighbor who's... hot," he told me, then shot Gina a look that was filled with *WTF...?*

She widened her eyes back at him and made a triumphant face that shouted *See! I was right!* But what exactly was she so victoriously right about? I was a little lost. If she'd brought up this mysterious new Hot Neighbor Guy to attempt to get Carl, I don't know, jealous...? It hadn't seemed to work. He was following the conversation with either one or both eyebrows raised, but other than that...? He didn't seem particularly perturbed. Of course Gina knew him far better than I did, and may have been able to read his interest in Henry in ways that I could not.

But then, weirder and weirder, I got even more confused as Gina looked over at me, caught me studying her, no doubt looking a tad perplexed. As she met my eyes, she immediately, instantly went blank. Completely expressionless. Like, deviously innocent.

No doubt about it, I was clearly missing something here.

She leaned closer to me, as if sharing a secret, and said, "I saw him last week. His real name should be *Red* Hot Neighbor Guy."

"Red is the color of the recently deceased!" Henry and Carl spoke in perfectly timed unison, and then all three of them cracked up.

"Oh-kay," I said slowly as I looked from Carl to Gina to Henry. Clearly, I'd missed something besides an orb from the spirit world and the hangry Ouija Board's message of *cake*. "You gonna share, or are you just gonna private-joke me to death?"

Henry had finally finished fussing with the food, and he joined us at the table. "Gina went to a séance last week," he informed me.

"*Really.*" I looked at Gina. She'd always brought her Ouija board to Henry's Halloween events, but I'd always thought it was a holdover from her childhood, rather than a sign of some crazy belief in the unknown. It was a toy—a weird toy, sure, but...

"It was research for a segment I'm producing," she explained, smiling at my disbelief. "I got the orb while I was there. It was fun. Right, Carl?"

I glanced around. Where was this oft-mentioned orb...?

"So much fun," Carl deadpanned. "The 'Spirit Guide' was named Pat. And every other word out of her mouth was..."

This time both Henry and Gina joined him: "Red is the color of the recently deceased!"

"Pat was a little over-the-top," Gina admitted.

"Any... thing... red show up?" I asked.

Carl looked at me. "You are adorable."

Gina ignored him and was shaking her head, answering me with, "Sadly, no. We didn't make contact with the spirit world because the dimensional portal failed to open."

Now Carl gave *her* a look. "You didn't *make contact* because there's no such thing as a ghost."

"That we know of." Gina clearly loved tormenting Carl. "And they prefer to be called *spirits*."

She got up from the table, and I glanced over to find Henry watching me, his expression somewhat pensive.

I gave him a *What...?* look—because something weird was definitely going on with him, but he just smiled and shook his head.

And then Gina distracted the crap out of me by putting something round and glass down onto the table.

"Boom!" she said. "The orb!"

"*That's* the orb?" I asked. It didn't look like much. Yeah, it had a glow that was vaguely blueish, but... As I picked it up, though, it turned bright green. "It's... like a... giant mood ring."

"That's exactly what I said." Carl nodded. "Orb from the spirit world, my ass. It reacts to the heat from your hands. Case closed."

I looked at it more closely and even shook it, holding it up to my ear, but it was silent—no rattle.

"Malcolm, show a little respect!" Gina chided me. "It's not a snow globe!"

Except as abruptly as it had gone green, it now turned a smoky white.

"That's weird," I said. "My mood ring never did that." I grinned at Henry. "Oh shit, am I dead?" I put the so-called "orb" back onto the table, hands up as I pretended to shy away from it in B-movie horror.

Shaking her head at my blasphemy, Gina gently picked it up and put it onto Henry's bookshelf where it glowered at us—an oddly ominous, angry white.

"Although, really, I shouldn't be worried unless it turns red, right?" I continued. "Kinda like Red Hot Neighbor Guy. Oh my God, maybe *he's* dead."

"Only if you kill him in a jealous rage," Gina said. Again, she was looking right at me, with this innocently sweet smile on her face, but her words didn't make sense. Was she talking to Henry again? *Kill him in...* Or maybe Carl...?

"What?" I asked, looking to Henry for help.

He was glaring at Gina again. "I'm pretty sure Gina got possessed by an idiot at that séance."

But Gina was oddly undaunted. In fact, she grabbed her handbag and her jacket and swept toward the door. "Will you look at the time? It's the bewitching hour! Carl, we must go!"

Wait, she was taking Carl *with* her...?

Carl sighed, but he got to his feet. He knew not to argue. "Nice meeting you," he told both Henry and me as he followed Gina out.

Henry scrambled after them, to walk them to the door, leaving me sitting at the now empty table, with the still-white orb glaring at me from its new home on Henry's bookshelf.

"What just happened here?" I asked it.

It didn't answer, so I had more cake.

CHAPTER THREE
Henry

Gina made kissy faces and noises at me as Carl led the way out the door.

Yeah, yeah, I knew what my mission was. Grab Mal and kiss him.

I was suddenly sweating, and probably a bit wild-eyed, so she hugged me hard and whispered, "He wants this, too."

He being Malcolm.

Except, she couldn't know that. Not for sure.

On the other hand, she'd rarely been wrong before.

Still...

Life with Mal as my friend was already pretty freaking great.

Life without Mal would suck.

But I was going to do this, because love was worth the risk.

I locked up, then went back into the living room to find Mal cleaning. He'd gotten several trash bags from the kitchen and was being careful to separate out the recyclables.

"You don't have to do that," I said. I'd pictured the two of us sitting on my sofa. I'd lean in and say something brilliant and witty before I brushed my lips against his in a less violent version of *Grab him and kiss him...*

But he was moving briskly and efficiently around the room—this would not work if I had to chase him down.

"The orb still isn't red," Mal told me, "so I'm guessing that the ghost maid isn't going to make it tonight."

I laughed. "No probably not." Okay I just had to say this. *Can we maybe sit down and talk...?* I took a deep breath.

"So tell me more about Hot Neighbor Guy," Mal said.

Who...? "Oh," I said. "Yeah. There's... really nothing to... He just moved into the rental, across the street."

Mal looked at me. "You gonna... How did Gina put it? Grab him and kiss him passionately? Or, maybe slightly more reasonably, ask him out on a date?"

I laughed awkwardly. "And break my forever-alone streak? I don't think so."

Ah, crap, by going for the obvious joke, I'd just blown a potential segue into the conversation I wanted to have. *Grab him and kiss him passionately? Funny, I was just thinking I should do that, not with him, but with you, cause you know, I've pretty much always been in love with you...*

Aaaaggghhhh!

One step at a time. *Can we maybe sit and talk...?* I took another deep breath.

Again, Mal spoke before I could. "Carl seems nice."

"Yeah," I agreed, because yeah, Carl *did* seem nice.

"Although, dating him could be a challenge," he said with a snort of laughter, "with Gina micromanaging, like a mad puppet-master."

Oh, my God. Really...? Was he...? I cleared my throat. "You, um, thinking about calling him?"

"Oh God no," Malcolm said, his response so swift that I knew it was genuine. "I don't need that drama. Besides, Carl's more your type."

And there it was. The conversational segue I'd been waiting for.

"Well, yes and no—"

"The cake was *really* good this year." Mal cut me off.

"Yeah?" I said.

"Definitely in your top three."

His praise for my cake was almost enough to distract me. But I got back on target, moving in front of the sofa, gesturing for him to join me. "Can we maybe sit for a minute and—"

Malcolm followed me over there, but cut me off again before I could sit. "Do you mind if I crash on your couch tonight? I've got an early appointment with a new client and all of the sugar in my system is about to make my eyes roll back in my head."

Since when did Mal have to *ask* before crashing on my couch...? It threw me for a moment. "Of course," I finally said and then went into a babble. "I have to be up early, too, to finish the photo edits for the Gorfney wedding."

Mal snickered. "I'm sorry, but what kind of name is *that*?"

I laughed, too, grateful to be back on more familiar ground. I reached out and nudged him. "Be nice."

He laughed and bumped me back in that way he'd always had of getting physical without *really* getting physical. It used to drive me crazy. But now it caught me off-guard and I tripped—probably over my own ginormous feet—and nearly fell on my face.

But Mal grabbed me to keep me from falling—and suddenly I was *exactly* where I wanted to be.

Held tightly in his arms, my body pressed completely against his, my mouth inches from his...

Grab him and kiss him! Grab him and kiss him! My heart was pounding and my brain was on fire. *He'd* grabbed me, which left it to *me* to...

But he was shocked by the sudden contact. Not shocked enough to let go. Or maybe he was *too* shocked to let me go. Kinda hard to tell.

"Malcolm, I—" I said the exact same moment that he said, "I think that—"

We both stopped, although he still didn't let me go, and I, of course, did not pull away.

"Oh, sorry, go ahead—" I said as Mal said, "No, you go first—"

I took the conversational baton—Gina would've been proud—although I couldn't manage more than a whisper as I told Mal, "Gina thinks my forever-alone streak would magically end if I just..."

And I did it.

It wasn't much of a kiss—or at least it wasn't in terms of traditional tongue-down-your-throat frenching. I didn't do more than softly brush my lips against Mal's—and yet it was everything. It was *epic*. My heart was in my throat. You hear that expression a lot, but I swear to God that it really was as I pulled back to look into Mal's eyes. God, I was terrified of his reaction—of seeing his pity or his amusement or... I didn't even know what.

But Malcolm's eyes were wide and stunned and he still didn't move and the spark of hope in my heart burst wildly into flame as I leaned in to kiss him again—

BAM BAM BAM!

Someone was knocking—pounding—on my front door. It startled us both, and Mal let me go, even as I stepped back, away from him, and away from him, and away from him even more.

"What the hell...?" I breathed, then realized, "Gina...?"

I headed for the front door on still-shaky legs, and threw it open, fully expecting to find Gina and Carl but...

There was no one there.

It was a quiet late-autumn night on my deserted suburban street. The Trick-or-Treaters had long since gone home. I could see the flicker of light from TV screens through windows as some of my neighbors embraced the concept of *Netflix and chill*.

But then, suddenly, there was an enormous clap of thunder.

"What the hell was that?" I asked the night, even as I slammed shut and locked the front door.

I waited for a moment, but the thunder didn't repeat. Neither did the knocking. Thank God.

I headed back to Malcolm and the still-fresh memory of that small but amazing kiss.

"I think the shenanigans part of Halloween has started, but I have no idea why it's suddenly thundering—" I cut myself off as I saw... "Malcolm...?"

He was fast asleep on my sofa.

What...?

He snored—softly but convincingly. Except I wasn't at all convinced that he was really sleeping.

"Oh, God," I said, "okay, you don't have to pretend to be asleep. We don't have to talk." He didn't sit up, didn't move, didn't say anything. So I kept going. "I shouldn't've kissed you. I'm sorry if I... made you uncomfortable." Oh, God...

Mal snored again, and I took that for what it was. He was either fast asleep or pretending to be—and neither was an even remotely positive response to a first kiss that I'd thought was epic.

I gently covered him with my throw blanket and, feeling exceptionally shitty, I went into my bedroom and shut the door.

Malcolm...?

It was dark when I woke up, but it was less dark than it had been for a long time—the light from the damned vessel casting a reddish glow in the little room.

I stretched cautiously, wiggling my fingers and toes, checking for cricks in my neck and other spots of pain. Nothing too bad—I was young and in relatively good shape. I *did* have to pee, so I staggered off to find a bathroom, taking a long drink of water from the sink while I was at it.

A quick look in the mirror, too—brown hair, green eyes, handsome face, full set of teeth—yup, this would do. Although I didn't have much of a choice, since he'd picked me. Probably didn't even know it, idiotic dumbfuck.

I went back into the living room to scope out the situation, figure out my next move.

The transfer had been as violent as its accompanying thunderclap had signaled, and it had knocked us both out. He—what was left of him—was still down for the count, snoring on the sofa. I could see him, but no one else would be able to. That would be funny as fuck to watch, but I wasn't about to stick around. I had places to go, things—and people—to do.

I picked up his—my—bag, a ridiculous day pack that I wouldn't be caught dead carrying, and immediately knew its contents—an e-reader and some paperwork for his—our—copy-editing service. God, what a shitty, stupid job.

"Nope," I said aloud. My voice was a rich baritone.

I dropped the bag on the sofa, at his invisible feet. If I'd put it down on top of him, he'd never be able to get up. Even I wasn't that cruel. Or maybe I was, but just not right now, in this moment of new-found freedom.

I was wearing a T-shirt and jeans, so I scanned the room for a jacket—found one draped over the back of a chair, put it on, looked down at myself.

"You've got to be shitting me." I took it off, dropped it on the floor. I found a pair of sunglasses—that was more like it. "Thank you." I could always pick up a jacket when I got to Vegas. I'd steal it if I had to, although…

I was carrying car keys, a cell phone, and a wallet—which contained both cash and credit cards—cha-ching. I re-pocketed everything but the keys, hitting the find-my-car button.

A chirp sounded from somewhere. I hit it again and followed it toward the front of the house.

"Let's get this party started," I said, turning to look, one last time, at my hapless host, who still hadn't awoken. Once he did, he'd never sleep again. "Not you, dumbfuck. You have to stay here. Forever. Have fun with that."

CHAPTER FOUR
Henry

I woke up later than I'd expected—to birds singing and the sun cheerfully shining in through a crack in the curtains. I grabbed my phone to check, and yes, it was nearly eight a.m. That was weird. The pipes in my house rattle when the shower goes on, and since Mal had said he was getting up super-early…

Mal.

My heart sank as I remembered last night's embarrassing disaster. And suddenly the day seemed a lot less bright. I got out of bed and threw on some clothes and cautiously crept out toward the living room.

The house was silent. I was pretty sure I was alone, and sure enough, Mal was no longer on the couch.

His backpack was still there, which was strange. It was Mal's version of a man-purse, and he carried it everywhere. I doubled back towards the bathroom, but the door was open and the little room was empty. He was not in the dining room, not in the kitchen… I opened the door to look out across the front yard, and the street in front of my house was clear. Mal's car was gone.

Or rather, *Mal* was gone.

So I called him on my phone. If I waited, it would only get harder and weirder, so I just clenched my teeth and did it. But the phone barely rang before Mal's voicemail picked up.

"You've reached Malcolm Goodman," the recording said. He was using his professional copy editor voice, and it exuded both patience and calm—traits I knew he had to work hard to achieve. "Leave a message and I'll call you right back."

"Hey Mal, it's me," I said after the beep. "You must've left early, and I know you're probably in the middle of that meeting, so no worries. I just wanted to let you know that your bag's here, in case you need it. Today's a running day for me, so I'll be out for about an hour." I took a deep breath. "I'm really sorry if I made things weird last night." I paused, not sure what else I could say, and finished with an inadequately moronic "Okay... Bye."

I winced as I hung up. That had not been pretty, but at least it was done. If there was any hope of salvaging our friendship, it had to start with my apology. And then I'd have to turn it into a joke. Hahaha, wasn't that funny when I tried to kiss you? What was I thinking?

God, *that* was going to suck—laughing with Malcolm about it, while in truth my heart was breaking and my dream was crushed.

I jammed my feet into my running shoes. For years, I'd fantasized a future where my life was completely and permanently intertwined with Mal's, but last night, reality had caught up with— and bitch-slapped—me.

I pushed my way out of the house, and hit the street, hoping my run would clear my head.

Malcolm

When I woke up, I had no idea *when* I was.

I knew *where*. I was on Henry's sofa, in Henry's living room, in Henry's house. And that made it okay—the oddly floating lack of knowing what day or month or even year it was. In fact, I just let myself lie there for a moment, remembering an awesome dream about... and just like that, as I attempted to focus on it, the memory vanished, the way dreams often do.

Henry had been part of it, that much I knew, and it had been lovely, but... Nope. Details gone.

With a sigh, I dug for my cell phone to check the time, but it wasn't in my pocket, which was strange.

That was when I noticed that it was awfully bright in there. Why hadn't my alarm gone off? I sat up too fast and the room spun. *That* wasn't good.

Henry had a wall clock and I ran—more like staggered—toward it. 8:23...?

"Shit, Henry," I called, "I needed to be out of here two hours ago! Why didn't you wake me?"

But right then, the world shifted and I nearly fell on my ass. Instead, I caught myself on the wall near the bookshelf.

"Whoa. That's weird. Hey, Henry? Are you home?"

Again, Henry didn't answer, which didn't necessarily mean that he wasn't home.

I moved slowly and carefully into the dining room—test driving my wobbly legs and feet. "Man. Something is not right. Henry…?" Still nothing.

I got up close and personal with the dining room built-ins—as if we were partnering in an intimate tango. I'd always liked them. The bookshelves spoke of an earlier, simpler time when furniture was expected to remain in the exact same place forever. Or they spoke of an architect who was cognizant of Southern California's propensity for earthquakes. Either way, they really worked for me.

Right now, they were a combination of ladder and crutch. I moved along them carefully, clinging to the shelves. Vertigo hit me again, and I hugged the shelves even tighter. As a result, I was face-to-face with a folder that someone—no doubt Henry—had stuck between two books. And from that folder, a picture peeked out. It was a photograph, of me.

As I looked at that picture of myself—I was about two inches from the damn thing—I thought, *Well, that's strange. Why does Henry have a file with a photo of me in his built-in bookshelves?*

There could've been a thousand reasons. I reached for the folder, and tried to pull it free, so I could see what else was in there.

But it was stuck.

Seriously. It was like pulling King Arthur's sword from the stone without the royal pedigree.

"Are you kidding me?" I spoke aloud. I'm usually not one of those weirdos who talks to himself—at least I hoped I wasn't. I mean, yes, I do believe that there were things that needed to be exclaimed over, loudly, regardless of whether one had company or not. And this current "right now" seemed to fall into that subset.

I pulled that folder with all of my might and…

I pulled it free, but it was insanely heavy, so it dropped onto the floor, where it opened, spilling a pile of photos—all of me—at my feet.

"What the hell…?"

Henry had taken them—I'd recognize his photography anywhere. They were nearly all candids, taken from a variety of trips we'd gone on over the years, although a few were from the session we'd done in his studio—back when he'd suggested that maybe if I had an official "author headshot," I might get my ass in gear and finish writing my own damn book.

(Spoiler: having a headshot didn't help. I've been stuck on Chapter Seven for nearly three years.)

Although… the photo on the top of the pile was exceptionally nice. I leaned over to pick it up, which was a mistake because I nearly fell over, onto my head. And when I finally steadied myself enough to reach for the damn thing, I couldn't get it off the floor. It was stuck there. Except it wasn't. I managed to peel up the corner, and it didn't stick—it was just insanely heavy.

Dropping it back onto the floor made me stagger, and I stumbled toward Henry's front door.

Was I high? Seriously. Something was wrong with me.

"Do not tell me you pulled some nasty Cosby shit," I shouted. "Henry…?"

But Henry didn't answer me.

I was pretty sure by now that he wasn't home—that he'd left me here without waking me, which was so unlike Henry, it didn't make sense.

I couldn't even text him with a *WTF?!* because I didn't have my phone. I double-checked my pockets. Or… my wallet…? It was gone, too. Along with…

"You took my car keys…? Really…?" I swear I didn't move, but the world around me tilted, and I lurched, hitting the wall near the door and sliding to the floor. "That might've been a good call. But I've got to get to that meeting."

I crawled over and tried the door, but it wouldn't open. In fact, I couldn't even turn the knob. "Holy shit. Did you lock me in…?"

Right at that moment, the door swung open, nearly hitting me in the face. I had to scramble back, which made me lose my balance again, and for several long moments, I lay on my back on the floor, looking, I'm rather sure, like an upside-down turtle, as Henry strode in. He was dressed in running shorts and a sweaty T-shirt. He closed and locked the door behind him, ignoring me completely as he blew right past me.

"Hey, Marathon Man," I said, as I somehow managed to sit up. I didn't risk more than that—I felt safer down here, closer to the floor. "Thanks a lot for waking me up. And what the hell did you put in that cake last night, because there's something really wrong with me!"

"Total disaster," Henry said from the dining room, and I scooted on my ass in his direction, about to say *What?* when I realized he had his cell phone to his ear.

"Yeah," he said to whomever he was talking to. "I did it. I kissed him, but then some kid prank-knocked on the door. And when I came back, he was asleep or pretending to be asleep—I'm not sure which is worse. But yeah, it's all bad, and he was gone when I woke up."

"Wait, what?" I was confused. "You kissed... who...? *When?*" Had Carl come back last night? I was pretty sure I would've remembered that, especially if he'd stayed overnight. Unless Henry's drug-cake had been extra super druggy...

"Uh oh," Henry said.

His voice was loaded with so much dire dread that I stopped scooting and sat, woozy. As I watched, Henry reached down to pick up the photos that had fallen onto the floor.

"Um, you remember last year," he said to Gina—he had to be talking to her, I mean, who else? "when I took that darkroom workshop and you were all *Why don't you make prints of that cute guy you told me you're still crushing on*, only I wouldn't tell you who it was, and..."

Henry jerked the phone away from his ear. I could hear Gina's voice—the strident tone but not her actual words—as she shouted at him.

"What do you want me to say, Gina?" he shouted back at her, his un-Henry-like annoyance heavy in his own voice. "Yes, I've had a thing for Mal since forever!"

I froze.

"Picture me," Henry continued, "projectile vomiting in the dorm bathroom, crushing on the crazy hot senior who's fucking holding back my hair!"

I forced my mouth and throat to work. "Wait, what...?" I mean, I knew it at the time, but he'd been so drunk he probably would've crushed on anyone who smiled in his direction, and it would have taken some time to wear off, too. But it *had* worn off, like more than a decade ago, after he'd gotten to know me. Or so I'd thought. Except, he'd just used the word *forever*...

Henry sat down heavily at his dining room table, still ignoring me. Like, completely. Had he missed seeing me when blew in?

"Yeah," he told Gina. "So, I now have a folder-full of really nicely developed old-school candid prints of Mal." He exhaled his exasperation. "No! They're not creepy! Anyway, I stuck the folder in the bookcase and forgot about it, but it looks like he found it before he left."

"Damn right I found it," I said from my spot on the floor. "But hello! I'm over here...?"

Henry didn't look at me—it was possible he was mortified at what I'd just overheard. My head was spinning from the revelation—although whatever was in last night's cake was definitely adding to that.

He stood up, leaving the photos on the table, and went through the doorway into the living room, telling Gina, "Because he dumped them all over the floor and then took off."

"Took off?" I said as I used the table to pull myself up to my feet. "I'm right here!"

Those photos were really very good—of course they were, Henry had taken them—but as I reached for the top one, it was again stuck in that spot. Stuck, I should clarify, in its *new* spot, on top of Henry's table. What the hell...? Henry had picked them up—all of them, at once—with no problem.

I used both hands, and only then could I manage to lift the top photo a little—but it was too heavy to hang onto and it fell to the floor. It didn't land with the anvil-like crash that I'd expected. In fact, it didn't make a sound.

"Yeah," Henry said from the living room. "Mal was out of here before I woke up. He's gone, his car's gone..."

I suddenly realized that if *I* was the *he* that Henry'd been talking about all this time, then I was also the *he* that he'd told Gina he'd kissed last night. And sorry, there was no amount of drug-cake on the planet that could've made me forget *that*. Or leave after it had happened. I wouldn't've been able to, because my head would've exploded. Just, *pppghhh!*

"Kind of weird that he didn't take his backpack," Henry continued.

"No. You know what's kind of weird?" I stumbled toward him, caught myself on the doorframe, and shouted, "*That I'm standing right in front of you and you're pretending you don't see me. Hey!*"

"Whoa," Henry said, his back still to me, "it's windy out."

I didn't notice any wind, but Henry didn't have the best hearing in the world, so I pushed myself off of the doorframe I was clinging to, launching myself toward him like a rocket.

I must've tripped, because there's no such thing as a personal force field, although I could've sworn that Henry suddenly had one, because I bounced off before I hit him, and I fell, hard, into the loveseat. Goddamnit! "What is happening...?" I shouted.

I *must've* tripped.

But despite all my flailing and tripping and falling Henry *still* didn't acknowledge me. I wracked my brain, trying to remember him kissing me and me doing something so awful and embarrassing that it warranted this incredibly non-Henry-like silent treatment. But I got nothing.

"Of course I left him a message," he told Gina as he continued to pace. "I'm starting to get really worried. He always calls back right away and... That's strange. One of Malcolm's photos..."

He went back into the dining room and picked up the photograph that I'd dropped on the floor. As I watched, still prone on the loveseat, he lifted it effortlessly and put it back atop the pile on the table.

"No, it's nothing," he said into his phone, pacing further into the dining room.

I pushed myself to my feet, focused on getting my legs to behave, and managed to stagger after him.

"Nothing?" I echoed him as I baby-monster-walked my way over to the table. "I can play your little *I'm Ignoring You* game all day." I tried to push the photo back onto the floor, but again it didn't budge. "Except this shit is heavy as hell..."

Again, it took two hands and all of my strength to push that picture onto the floor.

And when Henry paced back, he looked down at the photo, and again completely ignored me although I was standing *right* there.

"This weird thing keeps happening," he said into his phone. "I just picked up one of Mal's photos, and all of a sudden it's on the floor again."

I suddenly had to hold onto the table with both hands as the world again shifted. "Unless you really can't see me or hear me..."

Okay, now I sounded completely crazy.

But still, Henry didn't so much as glance at me—I had to give him props for his total dedication to pissing me off. He just turned and left the room, heading back toward his bedroom. I stood there, just clinging to the table.

"Yeah," I heard Henry tell Gina as he walked away. "I have to shower, get some coffee and clear my head." He listened. "Great. Come on over, anytime after dinner. And let me know if he calls you. Thanks, Gina."

I forced my legs to walk—I was getting better at it, but I know my gait still must've looked pretty strange—as I followed Henry into his bedroom.

"All right," I said as Henry sat on his bed to take off his running shoes and peel off his socks. "Game over, you win, okay? Just stop. I really don't remember kissing you last night. And I had absolutely no clue you had a crush on me—well, okay, I had a clue, but God, you know, it's kinda scary."

Henry finally turned towards me as he stood back up, but he still wouldn't look at me.

So I kept going. "I don't want to lose you as a friend, and that's the way it goes for me. You know that. I get involved, I fuck it up, I lose a friend."

Without a word—and still no eye contact—Henry pulled his shirt off, and stepped out of his running shorts. Which left him, you know, very naked.

"Um, excuse me...?" I said, staring in shock. Yeah, *that's* why I stared. Because I was shocked. Not because he was insanely beautiful.

It had been years since we'd gone together to a gym and changed in the locker room, and even then we hadn't done that very often because *me* plus *gym* equaled *nope*. (Hey, I'm not a total slug. I'm good with long walks out in the fresh air—in the mountains or on the beach. Just don't call it a *hike*, please.)

But right now, we were in Henry's room, just a few feet away from Henry's very inviting-looking bed, so I stopped staring and turned away, because damn, and I cleared my throat and tried again, since he hadn't responded to my WTF. "Why did you just...?"

As Henry silently walked past me, hurrying toward his bathroom, I waved my hands in front of his face, but he didn't flinch, didn't blink, didn't stop.

"You really can't see me," I realized as I followed. "What the hell is going on...?"

He closed the bathroom door behind him—in my face—and I stood there in his hallway, trying not to panic. "Am I in that freaky *Stranger Things* world? Were you just talking to Winona Ryder? *I will not be Barb!*"

CHAPTER FIVE
Still Malcolm

It had been a long fucking day, and Gina had just called, saying she was on her way over.

I paced in Henry's entryway. My ability to walk was not yet perfect, but it had greatly improved. I toyed with the theory that I'd had some kind of weird stroke, which also somehow made me believe that Henry couldn't see or hear me. Although… if that was the case, why was I still here? Why hadn't I been rushed to the hospital. Or maybe I had been, and I just *thought* I was still here…?

The doorbell rang, and I reflexively reached to open it, but of course I failed.

"That's right," I muttered. It was too heavy. "Shit."

But Gina generally used a doorbell as more of an *I'm here!* announcement than a *May I come in?* And since Henry knew she was coming, he'd unlocked the door, and she just walked right in. She was followed by her large friend Carl, who looked a little perturbed at her informality.

"Gina! Carl!" I exclaimed. "Please tell me you can see me! Because Henry can't and I think it has something to do with—"

"Hey." Henry had heard the doorbell and came out to greet them. He'd finally put on PJ pants and one of his nerdy Ts.

"How are you doing?" Gina asked. She moved right past me to hug Henry, while Carl nearly walked into me. I had to dance a bit to not get stepped on.

"Not too fucking well, if I'm being honest," I answered her, "since you can't see me, either."

"I'm still pretty freaked out," Henry told Gina.

"And FYI," I announced, "he just put those pants on five minutes ago. He spends way too much time naked."

"You still haven't heard from him?" Gina asked.

Henry shook his head. "Nope. I checked his Twitter, too, but his last tweet was the day before Halloween." He forced a smile in

Carl's direction. "Hey, Carl. Sorry about the drama."

Gina headed for the living room. "So let's see those photos you were telling me about."

Henry

Gina had arrived to show her support. She came right after work, which is why Carl was with her. Or so she said.

I think, in her mind, *Carl* was the person I should've tried to kiss last night. Oh, trust me, right up until this morning, she'd been completely on Team Mal. If I wanted him, then she was going to help me get him, however best she could. But that fact that Mal had run away after I'd kissed him was, in Gina's opinion, *Not. Okay.* Because, deep down in the ancient caverns of Gina-Land, Mal and I should've drifted apart after college, and Carl and I would be married, and the three of us would be besties and probably even live together when her husband, Jake, was off with his SEAL Team.

Frankly, that never would've happened, even if Carl *hadn't* taken a job in London right after graduation. Because sometimes you meet someone and there is such an immediate lack of spark, that they might as well be straight. They are instantly in that *never gonna happen* place. And I knew, upon seeing Carl again, that he'd landed there, too, as far as I was concerned.

I also knew he'd gotten hit with a ton of Gina's noise in the car on the way over. *But why* aren't *you attracted to Henry...? Maybe you* would *be if you got to know him...*

She'd tried to get us to sit next to each other on the sofa, and yeah, the guy smelled nice, but nope. Plus, I was worried about Mal—and not just about the state of our friendship. I was worried something bad had happened, because he hadn't even texted us back.

It was all I could do not to get up and pace as Gina flipped through the printed photos of Malcolm.

"Wow. These are nice," she said.

I pointed to my favorite—the portrait I'd taken for his author headshot. "That's the one that kept ending up on the floor."

Gina glanced toward the open doorway that led into the dining room, where the mystery had occurred. Although why we were focusing on this instead of heading out to search for Mal, I wasn't quite sure.

"And you said your windows were shut so there wasn't a breeze," she said, looking over toward the living room slider that led out to my patio. "Hmmm…"

Carl looked at me. "Wait for it," he warned.

"It sounds like you have a ghost."

"Which means I'm really in trouble because I know you've seen the movies." Carl said dryly. "I'm gay *and* I'm black. He's gonna kill me twice."

Gina ignored Carl and grinned at me. "You want me to call Pat?"

I blinked back at her, confused until she said, "Pat Bergeron, the spirit guide. I'm pretty sure she does exorcisms."

Carl shook his head. "No one ever wants you to call Pat. Malcolm's drama is human drama. You move around a room, you create your own breeze. It happens. Look into my eyes and repeat after me: *This train does not stop at Crazy Town.*"

"Carl's right," I said. "I was pacing. And this drama *is* very human. I kissed Mal; he freaked and he ran. I'm gonna call him again and apologize. Again. And then he's gonna call me, and everything will be back to normal, please God."

Malcolm

"Holy shit!" I said, standing there in Henry's living room while he and Gina and Carl sat on the sofa where I'd slept last night, but no one even blinked because they couldn't hear me.

Gina thought I might be a ghost, and that was insane, because ghosts weren't real.

And Carl was wrong, because this train had most definitely stopped at Crazy-Town, and I was now not only living there, I was the freaking mayor.

But as Henry took out his phone to try calling me again, I realized that this was my opportunity to listen for it to ring, and maybe find it and answer it from whatever hell dimension I was stuck in.

Except as I was scanning the room, looking for my familiar blue case, my eyes fell on Henry's bookshelf. And the orb.

The orb that was no longer blue nor green nor white. The now-*red* glowing motherfucking orb. And in the panicked depths of my mind, I heard an echo of Henry and Gina and Carl, from last night, in perfect unison: *Red is the color of the recently deceased!*

"Holy shit!" I said again as apparently, from wherever my phone was ringing—it definitely wasn't in Henry's house—it went to my voicemail.

Because Henry left me a message. "Hey, Mal, it's me. Again. I'm really sorry I overstepped. Just call me. Or Gina. Just, please, call *some*one so I know you're okay."

I spun toward them, nearly falling over again. "But I'm not okay! I'm dead!"

"Want a beer?" Henry asked Gina and Carl. "Or maybe cof-fee...? Oh, and I've still got some cake..."

"The orb turned red!" I announced. "I'm a motherfucking ghost!"

Of course they didn't hear me. They were having a normal low-key evening. Well, it was *slightly* off, because I was missing.

Missing because I was *dead*.

I spun in a circle, slipping into full freak-out mode as life calmly went on around me.

"I wouldn't say no to some coffee," Carl remarked.

Both he and Gina started to stand as if to go and help themselves in the kitchen, but Henry stopped them.

"I got it," he said. "Sit. You've been on your feet all day."

I had to jump out of the way, or he would've walked right into me—or God, maybe *through* me—and I managed to catch myself and not fall for a change. Instead, I followed Henry.

"How did I die?" I wondered aloud, even though I knew he couldn't hear me because I was *dead*. "Car crash! There must've been a car accident but oh my God, where's my body? Am I lying in a ditch? I must be lying in a ditch! Christ!"

You'd think you wouldn't be prone to things like fainting after you're dead, but my legs got really weak and shaky, and I stumbled and fell.

It took me a moment to reorganize myself, but like earlier, I felt safest closer to the floor, so I ended up crawling into Henry's kitchen.

He was loading a tray with his cake—apparently not a drug-cake after all—and plates and napkins and utensils.

"I'm lying in a ditch," I told him, as he took three mugs down from his cabinet and filled them with his ever-present pot of coffee, adding them to the tray, "and coyotes are eating my face or God, my balls, and you're serving cake! And yes, it's really, really good cake but... Oh my God, you don't know that I'm dead! *Oh my God, I'm dead!*"

Henry had opened the cabinet where he kept his sugar and creamer, but now he paused before adding it to the tray. "Wow, it's getting windy again."

He calmly picked up the tray and carried it past me toward the living room as I continued to melt down.

"But if I'm lying in a ditch," I called after him, using the kitchen cabinets to pull myself back to my feet so I could follow him, "being fought over by face-eating coyotes, then why am I here?"

My legs were back to working badly, but no one could see me so I didn't care. I staggered back toward the living room, where Henry was setting his tray onto his coffee table, and where Gina and Carl were helping themselves.

They were quietly, calmly polite and civilized. *Pass me a napkin, Gina. Thank you. Do you take sugar...? You're welcome.*

I was neither quiet nor calm. My knees gave out, and I clung to the doorframe, sliding back onto the floor. "Why am I here?" I asked again, more loudly this time and getting louder. "Why did ghost-me come to your house, Henry, to haunt *you*? Why? Maybe you *do* know I'm dead, ohmygod, was it murder? Those photos— were you stalking me...? You said that you kissed me but I don't remember. Is the reason I don't remember because there was poison on your lips? You, with your ceaseless digging in your yard. You say that you're gardening, but... Oh God, what if I'm not in a ditch? What if I'm buried in your back yard and instead of coyotes, snakes and slugs and worms are eating my face? *What does it matter because God, I'm dead, I'm dead! I'm dead—*"

"When did it get so windy?" Gina asked.

"It's been a really weird day," Henry said. "I just wish Malcolm would call."

I crawled toward Henry. "Except you're so worried. It wasn't murder, it couldn't be murder. I mean, I love you but you're just not that good of an actor and God, you're going to be so upset when they find my body. I'm so sorry that I died!"

I flopped onto my back with the realization that sooner or later

Henry was going to get the news of my death. And he was going to be devastated. Oh, dear Lord...

"You know, I think I *will* have some cake," Carl said.

"Just save a piece for Malcolm," Henry said.

I sat up. "Oh my God, you're so sweet, I can't believe I thought you murdered me, but I'm dead and I can't eat cake anymore, not ever again!"

I reached out toward the cake, attempting to snag some icing with my finger, but like everything else in this world, it was heavy and hard to move. I mean, it gave a little when I pushed, but my finger came away clean. I licked it anyway, but nope.

I then tried licking the cake, but it was not unlike licking a piece of porcelain. I could feel the bumps and ridges of the icing with my tongue, but...

"I can't taste anything! I'm dead and I can't taste anything and I can't eat cake! Is this hell? You'd think there'd be limitless cake in heaven. Limitless and delicious. Hell is no cake. *Hell is other people eating cake!*"

Because yeah, as long as I focused on cake I didn't have to think about the way that Henry's heart was going to break because I'd somehow—stupidly—gone and died.

CHAPTER SIX
Henry

It took a while for the wind to die down, but it had finally been silent for a while when Gina packed up Carl and headed for the door.

She hugged me in the entryway. "Try to get some sleep. I'm sure Mal will turn up in the morning."

God, I hoped he'd get in touch with me long before morning, but I nodded, because she meant well.

Carl knew I was even more freaked out than I'd been before they'd arrived. I'd honestly expected Mal to at least text me by now.

"In the meantime," Carl said, "I think it's safe to say you're not being haunted by ghosts."

Weird, that wind was back again, but only for a moment.

Still Gina—whose grandparents lived in Palm Desert—checked to make sure they weren't leaving in the middle of a massive dust storm. She cracked the door and peeked out but the night was quiet and calm.

They left, and I locked up. Checked my phone again—nothing from Mal. I put away the cake, cleaned up the dishes, then wandered back into the living room. The remote for the TV was on the coffee table, so I pushed ON and sat down on my sofa.

MSNBC came on and I settled in to watch the news.

Except, the TV turned itself off. All by itself. It was on, I was watching as I nursed the rest of my coffee, and then, just *click*, it was off.

Jesus, really…?

I sat up and pushed the button on the remote, and it sprang back to life.

But then, maybe ten seconds later, the TV switched off again.

"Fine," I said, giving up. I stood up and announced to the universe, "You win. This was a shitty day anyway. I'll change the batteries tomorrow."

And then I headed to bed.

Malcolm

Yeah, you guessed it. That was me with the remote.

After Carl made his laughably false statement about it being *safe to say you're not being haunted by ghosts,* I had a very brief resurgence of hysteria.

I lay on the floor in Henry's entryway for a bit longer while he cleaned up, but then pushed myself to my feet and followed him back into his living room as he turned on his TV and plopped himself down onto his sofa.

The bright side to my meltdown was that I'd finally figured out how to walk again as I'd thrown myself around the room. But now I had a problem to solve.

"So I'm dead, and you don't believe I exist," I told Henry as he continued to ignore me. And yeah, I wish I could say that I stood there, pondering the best way to attempt to make contact since he'd put the photos back into the file, and opening the file was impossible for me. So dropping that same photo onto the floor—again—was a no-go. But I cannot pretend that throwing all of my body weight into pushing the on/off switch on the remote was a carefully calculated move. Instead, I just got pissed off.

"How am I supposed to think with the television on?" I asked with a ton of snark in my tone as I stomped over to the coffee table and whaled on the remote.

I was as surprised as Henry was when the TV shut off.

Whoa! I could actually do that. Yeah, I was exhausted and shaking from the effort, but…

Henry leaned forward and—with one finger—pushed the button on the remote and the TV sprang back to life.

"I may be dead," I said, "but I am here, and we are going to figure out a way to talk about this, because I can live without cake, but I will not be a ghost that you just pass off as a breeze from your phone-pacing!"

And with that, I threw myself at the remote, and the TV went off again.

Which was when Henry gave up and headed for bed.

"Wait, no!" I called after him. "We were just getting started!" I chased him into his bedroom. "You need to go back so we can figure out a way to communicate with the TV remote!"

Henry turned on the lamp on his bedside table, and plugged his phone into its charger. Then he pulled off his T-shirt and shucked off his PJ pants.

"Why are you taking *off* your pajamas? I thought you were going to bed?" I asked in amazement as now-naked Henry answered my second question by climbing—naked—into his bed. "God, you're hot, I've always thought you were incredibly hot, but now I'm dead..." And trying to touch him literally repelled me—it pushed me away from him. On a scale from one to never-again-eating-cake, that seemed dreadfully worse.

Henry turned out the light.

"By the way, I'm not sleepy," I told him. "So that's another thing about being a ghost that nobody talks about."

I walked around Henry's room in the dark, thinking aloud.

"I can't eat cake." At least I wasn't hungry. Still. "I can't touch you." That force field thing was *not* my imagination. "I'm incredibly weak, I can't be seen or heard, my balance is a joke—so as far as being rewarded for leading a good life, I'm calling bullshit."

Across the room, Henry's breathing had evened and deepened. Had he seriously already fallen asleep...?

I sat down on the edge of the bed to look at him more closely, and yup. He was out.

"Jesus. This whole situation is obviously bothering you," I said.

But as I spoke, I pushed Henry's leg over just a bit, to make more room for myself, and I realized... "Wait a minute. I just touched you. I thought I couldn't touch you."

Had I been wrong about the force-field thing? Had I really just tripped and flailed and... I reached out again and didn't just push his leg this time. I put my hand on his calf.

No force field. I was touching him.

"What the hell?"

I scooted up closer to the head of the bed and with one finger—cautiously—I leaned in and lightly touched Henry on his cheek.

No force field. His skin was smooth and warm.

"Holy shit," I breathed.

He'd always woken up with notorious bedhead, but since he'd just gone to sleep, he still looked like daytime Henry. Except a lock of his hair had fallen onto his forehead, and I couldn't resist leaning even closer and pushing it back.

It was as soft as I'd remembered, and God, his eyelashes were so long and dark and thick against his cheeks, and I'm pretty sure I sighed and my breath even managed to move his hair.

But then, suddenly, his eyes opened—I'd woken him up—and my hand was rather violently pushed away from him.

"Ow!"

Yes, I'd smacked myself in my own face. The force field—or whatever—was again fully engaged, and my hand had been repelled, right into my own nose.

"Hello?" Henry called. "Is someone there?"

"Yes," I whispered, hoping...

Henry reached over and turned on the light. But he still couldn't see me—he looked right through me as he looked around his room.

Shaking his head, he turned the light off again, settled back into his bed, and closed his eyes.

My powerlessness and sense of overwhelm grabbed me by the throat, and I shouted in frustration. "*Ahhhggghhh!*"

Henry opened his eyes.

Yes. That's right, Henry. I shouted again, "*I'm right here! Ahhhggghhh!*"

But Henry closed his eyes and snuggled more deeply down into his pillows and blankets.

"So windy..." he murmured.

"Oh my God." I gave up. He fell asleep again, almost instantly. I knew, because I held my hand as close as I could get to his leg, and as soon as he was out, my hand dropped those last few inches, and I could touch him again.

I sat for awhile, taking as much comfort as I could from his warmth—being dead was fucking lonely.

But then I saw it. A bag of candy corn, right there on old Sweet Tooth Henry's bedside table—no doubt in case he woke up in the night and needed a sugar fix. It was open, and the candy was spilling out.

I went over to it, and discovered that—with enormous effort and painfully slowly—I could push the little candy pieces around on the table top.

"Let's see you ignore this," I muttered as I took several deep, bracing breaths and got to work.

CHAPTER SEVEN
Still Malcolm

I've never been particularly good at sleeping. I'm not sure if I wake up and then have to pee, or if having to pee wakes me up. Either way, my nights include a fair amount of walking to the bathroom and back, about an hour's worth of attempting to get comfortable again, and lots of mental list-making and worse-case-scenario planning.

Henry, however, does not have that issue.

He slept like a stone as I toiled with the candy corn, pushing the little pieces into an awkwardly short message: *M IS HERE!*

I have to confess that I spent some of the night attempting to eat a piece of the candy. I managed to lift it as far as my mouth and even touched it with my lips and tongue. I tasted nothing, and it was so freaking heavy and hard—at least it seemed that way to me—I was worried that a) it would be like chewing a nail to try to bite it, and b) even if I managed to swallow it, it would be as heavy in my stomach as it was in my hands, and I'd have to haul that ish around with me for the rest of my afterlife.

The sun had been peeking through Henry's curtains for more than an hour when his phone alarm went off.

"Finally!" I said, minutely adjusting the candy corn that dotted the exclamation point. "Here we go."

I sat back, expectantly, but Henry rolled over and picked up his phone without looking at the table—or my message. He turned off his alarm, but then scrolled over to look at his messages.

"Nope," I told him. "I didn't call or text, but if you look right over here—"

With a heavy sigh, Henry threw back the covers and got out of bed.

Yeah. He was naked. "Robe…?" I asked. "No…? Nothing…?" Awesome. Whatever. Now look at my message. M is, indeed, here, exclamation point.

But as Henry reached across his bedside table, across my hours and hours and *hours* of work, he didn't look down. He focused on grabbing a towel out of what I had to presume was a basket of clean but unfolded laundry, and then he...

I screamed. "*Motherfucker!*"

He'd dragged the damn thing across the little table, completely destroying my message.

I sank to my knees in despair. "*Fuck!*"

He seemed a little puzzled at the stray pieces of candy corn that had fallen onto his floor—he picked them up and tossed them in his trash—but it was my shouting that made him stop and cock his head.

"Wow. Still windy this morning," he said.

"Fuck," I said again—a defeated whisper this time—as he went to take a shower.

Still Malcolm

Henry opened the bathroom door to let the steam out.

I peeked in, and he was brushing his hair in front of the mirror over the sink, that stupid candy-scattering towel now secured around his waist.

"Oh, good, you're not naked," I said and came into the little room.

Henry set his brush down on the edge of the sink and took his toothbrush out of the mug on the counter. As he brushed his teeth, I seized the opportunity and—grunting and gasping as if I were an Olympic weight lifter, I pushed the hairbrush as hard as I could toward the basin of the sink.

"I. Am. Here!"

With one last gargantuan burst of strength, I made the damn thing finally slip over the edge, and it rattled down into the sink.

"Weird." Henry effortlessly picked it up and put it back on the sink top.

I was badly winded and seriously pissed. "Not weird! Scary! Be scared! I'm haunting you, bitch! And it's fucking hard to do."

I was glaring at him in the mirror—I could see my own reflection, so maybe the no-reflection thing only applied to vampires, and

I was a different kind of un-dead.

But right then, Henry looked up, directly at me, his eyes suddenly wide and shocked. "Malcolm?" he breathed.

I stared back at him. "Henry…!" Could he really see me in the mirror?

But he definitely didn't hear me. He whipped around to look for me, but I knew, for him, I was now gone. And when he turned to look back into the mirror, I could also tell that—again, for him—I'd vanished there, too.

"How did you see me?" I demanded. "See me again!"

But Henry couldn't make me reappear. He rubbed his eyes. Which clearly didn't help.

"Great," he said. "Now I'm hallucinating." He picked up his phone—it was leaning against his toothbrush mug—and checked for messages again. "Mal, where are you?"

"I'm right here," I whispered. "Right fucking here."

Henry

I had work to do.

I'd only spent a few distracted hours yesterday, sorting through the mountain of photos from the Gorfney wedding, and my promised deadline was approaching, fast.

So I sat on my sofa with my laptop on the coffee table in front of me, and tried to pretend I wasn't watching my phone in hopes of a text from Malcolm.

I'd barely gotten started when, to my surprise, the TV just suddenly went on.

The remote was on the coffee table—about two feet from me—where I'd left it last night.

"Really?" I said. I reached over and picked it up. I turned off the TV, then took the failing batteries out of the remote and set it all down in a pile on the coffee table. I'd replace them later.

That weird wind was back. I almost turned the TV on again—to check the weather channel—but the wind stopped almost immediately.

I checked my phone again—still nothing from Mal—before turning back to my laptop.

I was making adjustments on a really fantastic picture of the bride with her mother when my computer started glitching.

The screen started getting dark. Just all by itself. As if someone was leaning on the brightness control and dimming it.

I hit the button to make it brighter, and it did.

But then, almost immediately, it started dimming again. I pulled my hands away from the keyboard, in case I was inadvertently hitting some combination of keys that were a short-cut to the brightness control.

But nope, the screen just kept getting dimmer all by itself.

Enough of this shit. I wasn't getting anything done—I might as well use my time more productively.

I reached up and slammed my laptop shut, then grabbed my phone and headed out of the house.

Malcolm

You're right again. That was me.

I hit the power button on the remote, and then got all excited, you know, "Here we go!" when Henry picked it up. Except he stopped our little communication session cold. I couldn't even turn the TV off and on in some kind of pattern because he took out the batteries.

I may have shouted a little.

The wind! The wind!

That, too, was me.

But then I stood there and thought, *What the fuck else can I push?* Like, where's Gina's goddamn Ouija board when you really need it…? But she'd taken it home, so…

My brilliant plan was to use the brightness control on Henry's computer to get his attention, then maybe bring up some kind of Word or Pages doc, and hammer out a message, one exhausting letter at a time.

The button-pushing thing is one hell of a workout, by the way. I haven't exerted myself this much in years.

But Henry's response was to slam his computer shut—nearly catching my fingers, which really would've hurt. And of course there was no way I could open it again. Pushing a button was one thing. I could throw all my frustration and anger down at it. But pulling up a lid…? By my fingertips…? Nope. Never gonna happen. And then it didn't matter, because Henry left the house.

I sank to the floor, exhausted. "That's okay, don't tell me where you're going or when you'll be back. I'll just be here, waiting, for eternity. Kinda dead. Still very, very dead… And so fucking sorry that I never kissed you when I had the chance, God damn it…"

I heard Henry's car start from out on the driveway and then I heard him pull away.

And I put my head in my hands and let myself cry.

Still Malcolm

It was dinnertime when Henry finally returned—not that I was hungry on account of being dead and all.

But H came back into the house carrying a bag of take-out, and as he took it into his kitchen, I shouted a greeting from where I was lying, stretched out on the sofa.

"Honey, I'm home!" That was actually supposed to be *his* greeting to me. And then I answered him with, "How was *your* day, dear? I spent three hours of *my* day in the bathroom, leaving another message for you."

Henry came into the living room, carrying his dinner plate and looking somewhat grim.

I sat up, because he was heading for the sofa, and I didn't want him to sit on me and be repelled. Or maybe *I'm* the only one who'd be repelled by the force-field thing, and how would that work if I was underneath him? I didn't want to find out.

He set his plate on the coffee table, next to his laptop. As he sat down next to me, his phone rang.

Henry answered it, fast. "Gina! Hey! Any word from Malcolm?" Her answer was an obvious *no*, since I hadn't had the opportunity to *ghost* over to *her* house and write *her* a message in candy corn, and he instantly deflated. "No, me neither," he said. "Yeah, and I spent the entire day checking hospitals and—" he cleared his throat "—morgues."

I winced. "Ah, Christ, I'm so sorry."

"Nope," Henry said into his phone. "Didn't find him. No record of his car being towed or impounded either. Malcolm has vanished off the face of the earth."

"I'm right here," I whispered.

Henry sighed. "Yeah, I'm gonna be working late, because I didn't get anything done today. In fact, I better get to it. Talk to you later. Yeah. Bye."

He ended the call and tossed his phone onto the table. With another sigh, he opened his computer.

This time, I didn't mess with the screen's brightness.

I just sat with him while he ate and worked, wishing I could help but knowing there was little I could do that wouldn't make his shitty day worse.

CHAPTER EIGHT
Henry

The little road trip I'd taken that day had been exhausting. I'd hit every hospital in the area—not just the ones between my house and Malcolm's apartment.

And I went into each of them, knowing that privacy laws would keep the nursing staff from being able to tell me if someone matching Mal's description had been brought to the ER. But all of them managed to inform me that there had *not* been any new thirty-something white male John Does during the timeframe Mal had been missing.

Same thing with the morgues.

I let everyone know that Mal had been an only child, and with both of his parents passed, I was it. I was his family. I left behind my contact info—phone number and email address. And now I dreaded checking for messages, for fear of bad news.

Tomorrow's task would be visiting police stations and local jails. Maybe even filling out a missing person's report, because enough was enough.

I ate my dinner automatically, cleaning my plate without tasting a thing.

And I really don't remember nodding off, but I guess I did, sorting through photos of the newlywed Gorfney's sweetly romantic first dance.

I dreamed I'd fallen asleep in front of my computer while sitting on my couch. So much for my vivid imagination.

It was one of those dreams where I wasn't quite sure if I was awake or asleep as I felt someone shift on the couch beside me.

And then I heard Mal's familiar voice, as if he'd leaned in close and was speaking quietly, right into my ear.

"I'm here, Henry, but I can only talk to you when you're asleep."

I opened my eyes and looked, and God, yes, Malcolm was sitting right there, beside me.

But he wasn't smiling. He looked so serious—almost grim as he continued in that same quiet voice, "So I need you to stay asleep—"

"Holy shit!" I woke up with a start, and just like that, Mal was gone.

Malcolm

"No, just *shit*," I corrected Henry as the freaking force field pushed me back, away from him. There was nothing holy about *any* of this. "What part of *Stay asleep* is so hard to understand?"

Henry had jumped to his feet and was now looking wildly around the room, as if I might be hiding in the two inches of space beneath the sofa. "Malcolm, are you really here? Oh, my God, could I sound any crazier?"

I didn't know what to tell him.

But then, with a sigh, he said, "I gotta pee."

"Finally!" I said. I would've clapped my hands, but I was half-afraid he'd be all *Is it thundering now...?* "Seriously though, your bladder is ridiculously huge."

He headed out of the room, and I may have skipped a little as I followed him. Because now we were getting somewhere.

"Whoa! What the hell...?" I heard Henry exclaim.

I found him standing just inside the bathroom door, stopped short by the glory of my exhausting effort. Or maybe *glory* wasn't the right word.

It had taken me hours, but I'd managed to loop one now-limp streamer of toilet paper up and over the rod for the shower curtain, and then all the way back to the sink. It was actually a little embarrassing.

"Well, since being dead makes me ridiculously weak," I explained even though he couldn't hear me. "And toilet paper is slightly easier to move, partly 'cause of the roll... I know it looks like your bathroom has been TPed by a very small child who was raised by show poodles and has only read about Halloween pranks in a book, still..."

It may have been ugly and meager and seemingly lazy, but my embarrassment gave way to a surge of satisfaction that I'd finally gotten a message through. There was no way Henry could find excuses for this. This was not the product of the wind. It could not possibly have been caused by his relentless pacing, either.

"Stand in front of the mirror!" he yelled at the top of his lungs. "Maybe I can see you there!"

"You don't need to shout," I told him. "I'm dead, not deaf. Still, you're talking to me—that's an improvement."

I stepped behind him, and together we looked into the mirror. *I* could see us both, but...

"You still don't see me," I concluded.

Henry was frustrated and clearly feeling foolish. "This is insane," he muttered.

Still, he tried closing his eyes and opening them fast.

He turned his head to the side, then whipped it back around.

He ducked beneath the mirror, then quickly lifted his head...

He *did* look rather intensely insane, and I would've laughed if my own frustration levels hadn't been off the chart.

Henry shook his head in disgust. "I am definitely losing it."

He swiped at the streamer of toilet paper, jerking it down and wadding it up. Two and a half seconds to undo my entire afternoon of work. I sat on my urge to scream, mostly because if I got one more *Jeez, it's weirdly windy,* I might never stop screaming again.

Look-it," I said. "I hate suggesting this, because, well, on a normal, pre-dead day, I would never condone this shit, but, maybe you should call Gina and get the phone number of her Spirit Guide, Pat. Maybe *she'll* know why you saw me in the mirror this morning—and how we could get that to happen again. Or she might have suggestions for strengthening exercises, so I could train to pick up a pen and maybe in five or ten years I could write you a note...?"

As if on cue, Henry's phone rang. As he took it from his pocket, I saw Gina's name on the screen.

"Or, Gina could call *you*..." I added. And her call wasn't as much as "on cue" as it was simply Gina being Gina. I don't think I've ever been to a movie or out to dinner with Henry without his having a missed call from Gina when we were through.

Henry answered his phone as he savagely tossed the wad of toilet paper into the trash and went out of the bathroom.

"Gina," he said as I followed him down the hall. "Hey. I was just thinking about you. Remember that time you and Mal played that *hilarious* April Fool's joke on me...?"

"Ah, Christ," I realized. "Okay. You think we're pranking you. I would probably think that, too. But ask yourself this. Is it April? No. No, it's October. November, actually." Halloween had been two nights ago, which meant today was November 2nd. "Rabbit, rabbit," I added automatically, before it occurred to me that not only had I missed the November 1st deadline, but the good luck one could allegedly get from saying *Rabbit, rabbit* on the first day of the month probably didn't help those of us who were already dead.

Meanwhile, Henry was as close to snarling as I'd ever heard him. "I checked the morgues today, remember?" he told Gina. "We've moved *way* past funny. So if this is some kind of zany plan to get me to think my house is haunted so that I'll call Pat, the *Spirit Guide*—" his stress on the words put heavy air quotes around them "—and then Malcolm will pop out and everyone will laugh…? Ha. Ha. Ha." He punched out the words in a tone that had nary an ounce of humor. "Give me her fucking phone number. Let's get this over with."

Still Malcolm

Pat Bergeron, Spirit Guide, was going to squeeze Henry in with a house call that very same evening.

I tried not to get my hopes up as we waited for her to show, but I must admit that when the doorbell rang, I followed Henry to the door with hope-like anticipation churning inside of me.

"You must be Pat," Henry said as he opened the door to reveal a woman who, had she been food, would've been crunchy granola laced with some seriously high-quality weed. She wore a long skirt and a flowing jacket and she carried two heavy-looking bags that I assumed were filled with ghost-hunting electronics. Or maybe crystals and meditation chimes. But most likely they contained a combo of the two.

She was younger than I'd imagined, with reddish brown hair and a pretty face. I silently apologized to spirit guides everywhere, for assuming they all must be well into the crone stage of their lives.

"I'm Gina's friend, Henry," he said, stepping back to let her in. "Thank you for coming so quickly. I'm sorry it's so late."

"I do most of my work at night," Pat said in a pleasantly musical, alto voice, muscling her bags through the door and stepping aside so that Henry could close it behind her. "In fact, I've got an eleven-thirty in Burbank, so we'll have to move a little quickly."

"Of course," Henry responded with a straight face, as if everyone in the Valley knew that Burbank was particularly haunted. He reached for her bags. "Let me help you."

She surrendered her equipment completely, but then went rushing right past me, toward the living room. "I can definitely sense a presence coming from the back of the house!" she exclaimed, and— *poof!* All of my hope dissolved.

"This might be why no one takes you seriously, Pat!" I called after her before turning to Henry who didn't hear me, either. "How much are you paying her, because *no.*" I shook my head. "Nope."

I'm not sure what I was expecting—for her to step inside and see me? Or even if she didn't manage to meet my eyes, maybe she'd at least smile vaguely in my direction...? Yeah, that had been too much to ask.

I followed them more slowly into the living room, where it didn't take long for Pat to set up her gear—a computer and some high-end mics—as Henry sat on the sofa, grimly watching.

"The fact that you saw Malcolm in your mirror this morning is significant," Pat told Henry as she began scanning the room with an iPad in one hand and, yes, a crystal—ten points for me!—in the other. "Mirrors are windows to the spirit world."

"Really." Henry said. I knew he was struggling. Just a few days ago, I would've been sitting beside him, poking him, trying not to laugh at the idea that Pat-the-Spirit-Guide had come here to make contact with a ghost.

"Oh, yes." Pat was absolute.

And yeah, I know, we're not supposed to like being called *ghosts,* but what I *really* didn't like was not being alive, so call me whatever the fuck you want. It kinda didn't matter to me on account of being, you know, *dead.*

But Pat was right, mirrors *were* definitely *some* kind of window to *some*thing, because Henry had looked into his this morning and seen me. And I wanted more of that.

"It's obvious you're hosting a spirit who senses your concern for your missing friend," Pat told Henry. "It may have taken on Malcolm's form to catch your attention."

I was following her around the room, hoping she'd do *some-*

thing with her iPad and crystal that would make her notice me, but now I stopped and shook my head. "Or it may have been me..."

Henry nodded, but then exhaled hard as he rolled his eyes, and said, "Are you sure it's not... actually Malcolm?" And I knew he couldn't quite believe the words that had come out of his mouth.

I looked expectantly at Pat. Come on, Pat. Come on...

She made a face as she thought about it. "I'm... not picking up much of a male energy," she said.

I threw my hands in the air. "Of course not!"

"It's definitely a female spirit," Pat told Henry. "Or... a childish one. Yes, it feels to me like a... very *sad* little girl."

"Are you ever right about anything?" I asked. Again, she didn't hear me. No big surprise there.

But then she *did* surprise me by saying, "Whoever it was, moving those photos...? *That* would have taken tremendous, impressive effort."

"*Thank* you," I told her. At last, someone who understood at least *part* of what I'd been going through.

"This spirit is trying very hard to communicate with you," Pat told Henry, adding, "Let's begin. Please, take a seat."

She'd set up three of Henry's dining room chairs in a shallow U formation in the middle of the room.

Henry took a seat as Pat lowered the lights, plunging the room into a spooky dimness.

"Do we really need the dramatic lighting...?" I wondered aloud as I took the empty chair in the middle. "I'm gonna assume this one's for me, unless you want to save it for the *sad little girl...*"

Pat startled me by speaking in a much louder, more strident voice. "Are there any spirits out there willing to speak with us tonight?"

I looked from her to Henry, who had his eyes closed in frustrated agony.

I sighed—just a little, and quietly said, "Yes. Please. I'm here, and I need your help."

The two still-breathing people sat in silence. Henry opened his eyes and glanced at Pat. "Anything?"

Ah, Jesus. I spoke again, louder. "Yes. Please. I'm here, and I need your help."

Pat checked her equipment. "Nothing yet."

I stood up, in total exasperation. "I don't know why I thought this would work. *Shiiiiiit!*"

Pat leaned forward. "Did you hear that?" she whispered.

Henry was annoyed. "It's just the wind."

I looked at him. "Oh, yeah? The wind? *FUCK YOOOU!* Does the wind sound like this?" I got right in his face. "I'll give you a hint. *NOOOOOO!*"

Henry was unperturbed. "That's what I heard last night."

"Wind," Pat said. "Hmmm... But, is it actually windy outside?" I spun toward her. "Finally!"

"I didn't notice any significant wind when I was driving here tonight," Pat pointed out. "I think this might be something."

I ran over to Pat and shouted in her face. "*YEEEEEESSS!*"

"There it is again!" she said. "I think she's trying to speak to us!

"Still not a *she*, Pat," I said. "But you're getting warmer."

Henry was disgusted. "So, you believe the ghost—"

"Wandering spirit," Pat corrected him.

Henry blinked. "The *wandering spirit*. Is trying to communicate with us through... the *wind*...?"

"Through a wind-like sound," Pat said. "Yes. But we should test this to be sure it isn't some kind of strange feature of your house."

I started to laugh. I was so close but now... "What...?"

Henry shut that shit down. "I've lived here for years. It's not the house. Look, if this really is a spirit, we should ask it some *yes* or *no* questions. Like, one wind-sound is yes and two wind-sounds is *no*."

I gasped.

Pat spoke in her speaking-to-the-spirits voice, aimed somewhere up at the ceiling: "Do you understand that, sweetie?"

"Now we're talking!" I said, then bellowed. "*YEEEEEESSS!*"

Pat nodded. "That appears to be a *yes*."

"Great," Henry said. Then he, too, aimed his words upwards, as if I were flying around the room. "Now how about: *Are you Malcolm?*"

I ran—not flew—over to Henry. "*YEEEEEESSS!*"

"That's strange." Pat was peeved. "I was *certain* the spirit was female."

"Let that go, Pat!" I said.

"We should ask an obvious *no* question," Pat advised, "otherwise we can't be certain..."

Henry sighed. He was hating every second of this—which I took to mean he was unhappy that I was dead. "Okay," he said. "What's a good *no* question for Spirit Malcolm?"

Cricket's chirped. Tumbleweeds rolled. The clock ticked silently as I looked from Henry to Pat and back again.

"Jesus Christ," I finally broke the silent. "Am I a donkey? Is two plus two five? Do clouds make the wind blow? Come on!"

"I've got it!" Henry said, then again aimed his words at the ceiling. "Are you straight?"

"Finally," I said. "*NOOOOOO!*"

No one said or did anything again, until Pat finally shifted in her seat. "Well, that was a *yes*, so…"

"Shit!" I said. "I mean *NOOOOOO!*" This time I paused only briefly. "*NOOOOOO!*"

Pat was excited. "There it is! That's a *no!*"

Thank God. "My bad," I said.

But then Henry leapt to his feet like a defense attorney in a bad courtroom drama. "Okay, Mal," he announced loudly. "Game over! We've got it all on tape so you and Gina can tease me mercilessly until the end of time! You can come out now!"

Both Pat and I were taken aback.

"What," I said, "wait, no! All that effort, and you still think this is some kind of *prank…?*"

Pat was more prepared for this. "Oh," she said to Henry in a resigned tone, heavy with her disapproval, "you're a nonbeliever."

Henry turned to face her. "With all due respect, Pat, I'm pretty sure my friends are using you to set me up."

Pat smiled. "Sadly, I encounter more of you than I do wandering spirits like Malcolm. I hope you won't mind if I continue my conversation."

"Go crazy," Henry said. "I don't know how they're doing the whole wind thing…" He was looking at the ceiling again, this time searching for… speakers or…? I wasn't sure what.

"Malcolm, are you still there?" Pat asked.

"Yeah," I said tiredly. "I mean, *YEEESSS!*"

"I imagine this is upsetting for you," Pat said. "Are you upset, dear?"

I sank down to the floor. "*YEEESSS!*"

Henry laughed. "Oh, *he's* upset. *I'm* the one being punked."

"Do you know when or how you died, dear?" Pat asked me.

"*NOOOOO!*" I shouted, adding, "Although that whole Henry-murdered-me theory is back on the table. *NOOOOO!*"

"Do you know why you're here, why you haven't moved on…?" Pat asked.

"*NOOOOO!*" Now the look on Henry's face was a mix of rage and pain and I had to turn away as I tried not to cry. "*NOOOOO!*"

"Do you remember attending a party here on Halloween night?"

"*YEEESSS!*" I shouted.

Pat nodded. "But you died, shortly after…?"

"*YEEESSS!*"

"That's enough." Henry's voice was sharp. "This isn't funny!"

"*YEEEEEESSS!*" I said as loud as I could.

"Malcolm agrees," Pat pointed out. "I know you're struggling, Henry, but Mal came to you for a reason. He may not yet know what it is, but—"

Henry had had enough. "I'm sorry, no. Mal's *not* dead. That's just not possible. I think… I think you should go."

He was nearly quivering, he was so upset.

Pat sighed as she started unplugging her equipment, and Henry went to help her. They worked in silence, and then Henry carried both of her bags to the front door.

I trailed behind them, and I could tell that Pat had something more to say and was trying to decide if she should risk Henry's wrath.

It wasn't until he opened the front door that she made up her mind. In fact, she reached out and pushed the door shut, surprising us both.

"I have to warn you," she told Henry, "my schedule is extremely heavy this week. The fact that I had this current time-slot free on such short notice was sheer luck—or perhaps not, perhaps it was fate…" She drifted off for a moment, caught up in that possibility.

Henry shifted impatiently as he opened his mouth to reply, but she snapped to and continued, back to her no-nonsense tone.

"You've still got fifteen minutes left in your session, already paid for. Why not let me use that time to help you—or more accurately, to help *Malcolm*."

I nodded. Yes, please…

"I feel certain you're not going to be able to handle this on your own," Pat told Henry, "and the earliest I can squeeze you into my schedule is a week from Thursday, at four AM."

"No, thanks," Henry said. "I'm good."

He started to open the door, but she shut it again.

"You *are* going to call me," she told him. "But… Between now and then, when you find yourself floundering, the *Crimson Book* is a useful resource. It's pricey, I know, but the e-book is more economical. You can download it from my website."

Henry swallowed his reaction—his eyes were filled with *Are you fucking kidding me*—and instead he nodded politely. "Sure," he said, clearly willing to agree to damn near anything to get her to leave. "Yeah, right, if I need any more help, I'll buy your e-book."

This time when he opened the door, I stepped forward, trying to keep Pat from leaving.

"Pat, please don't leave me," I begged.

Pat stopped—had she sensed me…? But then she turned and called back toward the living room, "I'm sorry, Malcolm."

"Yeah," I said, "I'm over here, but okay…"

"I must respect Henry's wishes," Pat called, her back to me. "You'll have to gather your strength and convince him that you're here through other means. I wish you peace, and safe passage to the next dimension."

I held up two fingers in a peace sign. "Back at you, babe," I told her as she lugged her equipment out of the house.

Henry shut the door with quite a bit of force, then dug for his cell phone in his pocket, dialed it, and with his phone to his ear, he stormed back toward the living room.

He wasn't the only one who was pissed, and I stomped after him.

"Gina, hi. It's me," he said as he scanned the ceiling and the exposed wooden beams. "Please tell Malcolm that *that* was *bullshit!*"

"Oh. Yeah." I agreed. "That *was* bullshit. Pat could've helped me and *you made her leave!*"

And yeah, the "wind" was back, and since I was screaming in Henry's face, it was surely noisy as all hell.

Henry was livid. "Okay, this game's over."

Game…? Had he really just called this… My head exploded. *"This game is not over because it's not a game!"*

Henry was back to searching the beams and the ceiling, almost frantically now. "Where'd he put the speakers, Gina?" He paused only briefly. "The *speakers* that make it sound *windy*, which is supposedly *the dead voice of dead Malcolm*, and let me tell you right now, I'm *done!*"

"You're done?" I shouted at him. "YOU'RE *done…? You're DONE…?!"*

Now Henry was furiously redialing his phone as I paced the room, looking for something light enough to throw.

"You can't hang up on me, Gina!" Henry shouted. "I'm hanging up on you!"

"HANG UP ON HIM, GINA!" I screamed as loudly and windily as I could. *"YOU SHOULD DEFINITELY HANG UP ON HIM!"*

"And yeah," Henry said to her, "maybe I've known you forever, but going along with this fucking awful, hurtful, *stupid* prank just because I made the mistake of kissing my best friend, well… that's just *cruel!"*

"CRUEL?" Was he fucking kidding me…? *"CRUEL…? CRUEL WAS SENDING PAT HOME BEFORE SHE COULD HELP ME! CRUEL IS THINKING I WOULD DO SOMETHING TO YOU THIS STUPIDLY CRUEL! CRUEL IS ME NOT KNOWING YOU WANTED TO KISS ME UNTIL AFTER I WAS DEAD! ARGH!"*

I threw myself at Henry's coffee table, and to my total shock, I managed to sweep the contents—books and papers and even his dinner plate and fork—onto the floor with an enormous crash and clatter.

Henry and I both froze, staring at what I'd just done, and the sudden silence was deafening.

Henry's phone slipped out of his hand—Gina had long since hung up—its protective case bouncing once on the floor. Henry followed it, sinking down as if his legs could no longer hold him.

I crumpled, too, beside him.

"Please don't be dead, Mal," Henry whispered.

"Oh, God…" I breathed.

Henry closed his eyes and drew in a long breath, then asked, "Is it really you?"

My heart broke. *"YEEESSS."*

Henry sobbed his exhale, then gulped in another breath. "Are you really dead?" he breathed.

"YEEESSS." Oh, God… "I'm so sorry," I said.

Henry started to cry.

And I cried, too, unable to comfort him.

CHAPTER NINE
Malcolm

Time got a bit blurry. Not because I'm dead, but because I was so upset.

Imagine, if you can, if the man who was the most important person in your life was weeping in a heap on the floor—and you couldn't do anything for him. You could only sit, helplessly, powerlessly, and watch him cry his heart out.

Turns out ghost-tears-and-snot vanish completely when they're wiped away. (No real surprises there.)

So yeah. I lay there with Henry, on his living room floor, until his ragged breathing evened and slowed. But then I sat up because, Jesus, had he really fallen asleep...?

Insomnia had pretty much been my middle name since, oh, forever? Or at least since I'd stopped drinking-to-sleep, i.e. drinking until I passed out, which really wasn't the same as *sleeping*, when you compare it, apples to apples.

I'd often teased Henry about his ability to do something he called *combat nap*. He could lean back, even on an uncomfortable chair, and fall asleep close to instantly—and awaken in five minutes, completely refreshed.

But as I looked at him there on the floor, I knew he was a stiff-neck waiting to happen.

Also...? He was *asleep*, which meant...

I reached out carefully, still wary of the potential force field. But the no-force-field-when-Henry's-sleeping rule was in effect, and my hand made contact with his shoulder. I leaned in and spoke to him in as calm and quiet a voice as I could manage.

"Don't wake up," I told him. "Stay asleep but listen to me. I have a lot of questions, too. I don't remember dying; I don't remember kissing you, which sucks because I'm pretty sure I would've kissed you back." I probably wouldn't have admitted that if he was awake—or if I wasn't dead. But since he *wasn't* awake and I *was* dead, all bets were off. I added, "The orb is red now, by the way."

He hadn't noticed that yet, and it somehow seemed important.

Henry shifted slightly, his eyes still tightly closed. "This'sa stupid dream..." His speech was slurred, but he sounded indignant.

It was so very Henry that I had to smile. "Yes, it *is* a very stupid dream," I agreed, "but let's see how much you remember when you wake up, okay? Because I don't know what I did to make you see me in the mirror, and really, even if we *can* duplicate that, making faces at each other is *not* the way I want to spend my time here in the afterlife."

Henry lifted his head to look at me. His big blue eyes were unfocused but filled with fresh tears. "I don't want you to be dead." This time his voice was crystal clear.

My heart twisted in my chest as I pushed his hair back from his face. "Yeah, I don't want that either," I whispered, "but here we are." I couldn't help myself, and I leaned in and kissed him as gently as I could—and God, it was sweet—but yeah, he woke up at that. And the fucking force field pushed me back. And I was invisible to him again.

Henry looked around wildly. "Mal!" he called. "Malcolm...?"

"I'm here," I exhaled on a sigh, but of course he couldn't hear me now.

"I dreamed that you kissed me," he said, and I was just about to do the one-wind thing with a bellowed *YEEESSS,* when he added, "God, I'm so tired, I'm dizzy."

So I stayed silent, in hopes that he'd crawl into his bed and fall unconscious. Next time, I'd keep my message on-point—no distracting kisses, no matter how tempting.

And sure enough, he pushed himself to his feet and staggered off to his bedroom.

I waited there in the living room, hoping he'd do his Henry thing and quickly and easily fall asleep.

Henry

I was a mess.

I lay there, in my bed, in the dark, physically ill at the idea that

Malcolm was really dead.

Although... the alternative was that he'd sat there, laughing and enjoying the "joke," as I'd cried my eyes out on my living room floor.

So if Mal wasn't dead, he was, like, the world's biggest asshole.

Unless he was only trying to make me *believe* that he was the world's biggest asshole so that I'd fall out of love with him.

As I lay there, eyes wide open, I grabbed onto that possibility with both hands, like Jack's grip on the floating door as the Titanic sank. (That analogy made better sense to me at holy-crap o'clock in the middle of the night. But I bet you know what I mean. There was some intense stupidity happening for both Jack and me.)

Somehow—Gina—Mal had found out that I was hoping to nudge our platonic relationship toward the romantic end of the friendship-scale. And he panicked. And instead of sitting me down and giving me a gentle *Let's just stay friends* speech, he'd created this elaborate Halloween-themed, high-asshole-factor prank, meant to dissuade me of ever thinking about him romantically again.

And stupid, stupid me. Instead of thinking, *Jesus, Mal's a shithead*, my fucked-up brain had dreamt that he'd kissed me. Tenderly. Gently. Lovingly.

He'd kissed me and...

Smiled. He'd smiled at me and said... *Yes, it is a very stupid dream, but let's see how much you remember when you wake up, okay?*

"The orb!" I exclaimed. In my dream, Mal had said something about the orb being... red...? I leapt out of bed, grabbing my phone from its charger as I raced into the living room.

"Where the hell is that thing?" I asked aloud as I looked around, trying to remember where Gina had put it... On the bookshelf!

There it was.

And—holy shit—dream-Malcolm had been right.

It was glowing brightly red.

"Oh, my God..." I quickly scrolled through the recent calls on my phone, and found Pat's number and dialed.

It went straight to her voicemail: "You've reached Pat Bergeron, leave a message! Peace!"

"Pat?" I said, my voice cracking. "It's Henry—Collins. You were right and I apologize. I'm really, *really* sorry. Malcolm and I need you. Badly. So if you can fit me in before next Thursday, please do, and if not, I'll see you then."

I ended the call and rushed over to my computer, opening the laptop and Googling *Pat Bergeron, Spirit Guide.*

Her website came up right away—complete with obnoxious auto-play new-age music, all Tibetan drums and ocarinas and chimes. I swiftly muted it and said—aloud, in hopes that Mal's wind-noise speakers had mics that picked up everything, "This is where, if this *is* a prank...? You'll jump out and mock me for the rest of my life."

There, on Pat's oddly normal-looking, blue-sky-themed home page was a link for the book she'd mentioned: the *Crimson Book.* I hit the link for the e-book edition, and leaned in closer to read the page...

"Because this is where I spend—holy fuck! Seven *hundred* dollars...? On an e-book...?" My voice went up an octave. "Are you fucking kidding me...?" I took a deep breath. "Okay, but see, I'm doing it. See?" I spoke loudly and clearly for anyone listening in. "Visa card, name: Henry Collins. I'm typing in the card number, expiration date, January... And I am now hitting enter, and my credit card is being charged seven fucking hundred dollars because you've convinced me that you're dead and you're haunting me and I will live—gladly—with your mockage til my own dying day. Just please jump out at me now, Mal, *please*..."

Malcolm

I could not jump out at Henry—at least not in any way that he could see.

"I wish I could," I whispered as the clock ticked.

He'd come running out of his bedroom, surprising me—and not just because he was stark naked again. He'd remembered at least *some* of what I'd told him while he'd been asleep. So things were sort of looking up.

"Okay," Henry said, after he'd waited long enough and nothing had happened. "I just bought a seven-hundred-dollar e-book. Let's see what it can tell us."

I leaned in to look at the e-book he'd opened on his computer screen. "Oh, my God, it has infinity pages?" How could a book with infinity pages have a table of contents—and yet it did. "Ooh, you can input search words..." I pointed to the screen.

Henry was already over there, narrating as he typed, "Spirit... communication..." He hit *search* then leaned in to look. "Uh-oh."

I read aloud: "Seventeen million four hundred and thirty thousand pages of info for *spirit communication*." This might take some time...

Henry scrolled down the list, stopping on "*Spirit communication, comma, spells*. Whoa, really...? This book has spells...? Like, *spells*?"

He clicked that link, a new page opened, and something that looked like a recipe with an attached poem appeared.

"Okay, let's do this," Henry said. He raised his voice slightly. "Malcolm, stand in the middle of the room."

I did as he asked, uncertain as to what we were doing, but whatever it was, maybe he wanted to put on pants first...?

But no, apparently, pants could wait. Henry clapped his hands three times and spun in a circle as he chanted, "*Though the night is dark and the sun is bright, I bid you to dance unto my sight.*"

I was standing there, thinking, *You certainly are a dancing sight, spinning like that, Mr. Naked*, when all at once, I started moving. It was the weirdest freaking thing—as if my legs suddenly had a life of their own.

I looked down at me feet. Was I...?

Oh, my God, I was Irish Step Dancing!

"Oh no. No no no no no," I shouted.

But I could tell that Henry still couldn't see me, and he verified that by saying, "It didn't work."

"The fuck it didn't!" I yelled, stomping my way merrily across the room. "Make it stop!"

Henry made it stop—but only by casting other spells.

I went from Irish Step Dancing to singing operetta—Gilbert and Sullivan: "And so do my sisters and my cousins and my aunts, make it stop, make it stop, make it stop!"

I went from that to only being able to *dit* and *dah* in Morse Code—which, same as the step dancing and the rapid-fire lyrics to H.M.S Pinafore, I automatically, magically knew.

"Dah dah, dit dah, dah dit dah, dit." A tad wild-eyed, I spat out *make*, then *it*. Then *stop*.

I was released from *that* and plunged into the silent world of

ASL, which was kind of cool. *For the love of God*, I gracefully signed, *make it stop!*

Next on Henry's list was...

"Oh-nay! Oh-nay! Ut-way the uck-fay, Enry-Hay?" I would've been okay with the ridiculousness of Pig Latin, if Henry had been able to see and hear me. But he still couldn't.

From there we went to... "What genius put *this* on the list as a form of communication...?" I asked as, suddenly brightly lit, I made shadow animals against the living room wall—a rabbit, and then a dog, then what the fuck was *that?* A kangaroo...?

Then I was back to dancing—leaping and spinning without any skill, just basically emoting my ungraceful ass around the room. "Interpretive dance?" I shouted. "Interpretive fucking dance? Good thing I'm dead, cause I'd have to kill myself!"

Henry tirelessly moved down the *Crimson Book's* list.

One spell made me speak in fluent French. "Quels sont vos mots clés?"

I asked. What are your search words, or more literally, *your keywords?* "Peut-être, au lieu de *communication*, essayez... *connexion*, ou... *apparence...*"

I kind of liked that one. *Maybe, instead of* communication, *try... connection, or... appearance.* I sounded sexy, but that was moot because Henry still couldn't hear me. Or see me.

We moved on, and I was suddenly a mime, trapped in a box. I couldn't speak, but if Henry had been able to see me, he would've known, just from looking into my eyes, that I was now dead inside, too.

"What am I doing wrong?" Henry asked.

Of course I could not answer him, but Jesus, this was not the time to leave me here, in mime-mode, possibly forever...

He leaned in to read something from the screen. "*To break a simple spell be sure to utter* Ut det vobis dimittere—I grant you release."

His words did the trick and with a gasp—"Oh, thank God"—I broke free from the mime-box.

"*More advanced spells require spell-specific releases.*" Henry kept reading as I looked over his shoulder at the list.

"Ooh," I said. There was one, close to the bottom, that was in a red font, which according to the color code meant it was one of those more advanced spells. Each item on the list included a teaser of the spell's language in italics. "This one says *Bring you to me.* That looks promising."

As that old bit of wisdom from Nietzsche goes, *What doesn't kill you makes you stronger.* And since the mime thing hadn't killed me...

I gathered all of my new-found strength and jumped on the link to that advanced spell, and the page opened obligingly.

Henry was startled and he sat back, but then leaned closer to his computer screen.

"A binding spell," he said. "Hmm. We'll need... salt."

"And pants," I pointed out, as Henry headed—naked—toward his kitchen.

He returned momentarily with the round salt carton, but still completely bare-assed.

"No-pants works, too," I said. "It's not like I haven't seen every part of you at this point."

Still, the fact that Henry was naked was a very loud message. He did *not* think I was real. If he'd honestly believed I was there in the room with him, he would've been dressed. So... why was he doing this?

I decided not to care—and just be grateful that at least part of him was willing to try more of these spells. I knew that they worked—to some degree. They just didn't do what we needed them to do—to make Henry see and hear me.

But maybe this binding spell would do the trick.

As I watched, Henry poured the salt in a circle around him on his living room floor. He pulled his laptop closer so he could read the screen from where he was standing.

"Okay," he said. "Let's try this." He took a deep breath and exhaled hard. Cleared his throat. "*I bring you to my consciousness.*"

A low-pitched noise started—a hum. It was barely discernable, but it was definitely there.

"This is new," I said.

Henry closed his eyes, his face tilted toward the ceiling, his arms outstretched. "*I bring you to me.*"

The humming sound intensified, and I was pulled—somewhat violently—into the circle. "Whoa!" I shouted.

But Henry still didn't hear me. He did, however, raise his voice to be heard over the still-growing hum. "*I bind you to me as I bind myself to you!*"

There was a blast of light and it knocked both of us out of the salt circle and onto our asses as the humming sound crescendoed with a crash, then stopped.

A sudden wind—a real one, not the Mal's-angry wind-noise—blew the salt on the floor, breaking the circle.

I sat there, staring at Henry—who was staring back at me!

"Mal!" he cried as he lunged toward me.

Henry could see me!

"Careful," I said, but my warning was unnecessary. The force field was gone, too.

Henry wrapped his arms around me and pulled me in tight.

"You can touch me! And I can touch you!" I couldn't believe that we'd done this! "I couldn't touch you unless you were sleeping and—"

Henry pulled back to look at me. "Are you really dead," he asked, "or were you just, I don't know, temporarily invisible?"

What? "*Temporarily* invisible…?" I repeated.

"I mean, you're back," he said. "Maybe you're really back! Like not-dead back!"

He grabbed me by the hand and pulled me up and through the dining room, towards his front door.

He let go of me in order to throw the door open, clearly about to rush outside in his best Scrooge-on-Christmas-morning imitation, but I jumped in front of him.

"Pants! Pants!"

"Oh my God!" Henry finally realized, coving himself with his hands. "I'm naked."

"You are correct."

He ran toward his bedroom, while I attempted to close the open door.

But I couldn't move it. It was still heavy as hell.

"Ah, shit," I said. "Henry…?"

CHAPTER TEN
Henry

Completely overwhelmed—and okay, yes, panicked—I ran into my bedroom and slammed the door shut.

I stood there, breathing hard, knowing that I'd come in here for a reason, but completely unable to remember what it was.

"Please don't get your hopes up that I was only *temporarily invisible*," Malcolm called to me through my closed door, "because everything is still really heavy and hard for me to move, so I'm pretty sure I'm dead."

No, no, no-no-no. I flung the door open, and as Mal looked down at me, exasperation flashed in his eyes. "Really?" he said.

I remembered then. I was naked. I'd come in here to put on clothes.

But as I stared at Malcolm, getting dressed dropped in priority. Was he really here?

Or was I hallucinating...?

I poked him. Hard.

"Ow!" he said, adding as if he'd read my mind, "I'm really here but it's impossible, well, not *impossible*, but it's still extremely hard for me to lift things or open and close doors—"

I pinched him on the arm.

"Ow!" Mal pinched me back, on my arm.

This time we both said *Ow*.

"Why did *you* just say *Ow?*" I asked him. "*You* pinched *me*."

"Yeah, well, it hurt me, too!" Mal told me.

"How can you be dead," I asked, "if you can still get hurt?"

I pinched him again.

"I don't know. *Ow!*" Mal said. "Stop that!"

He pinched me back, and again, we both said *Ow!* But this time, I managed to jump back, and I stumbled and stubbed my toe, too.

Again, we unisoned an "Ow!" and both hopped around on one foot.

It was almost funny—and it certainly would've been if Mal wasn't insisting that he was dead.

"Nice," he said, laughing his disgust. "So *that's* a new fun rule. You get hurt and I feel it, too."

"You're actually here," I said, but I was really just seeing what those words would sound like if I said them aloud. I didn't honestly believe it.

"Yes," Mal told me firmly. "Put on some pants. Sneakers, too, Clumsy. Let's not do that again."

I looked at him and realized... "You're still wearing the clothes you wore on Halloween..."

Green T-shirt, jeans, his beat up sneakers... God, he looked good.

"Believe it or not," Mal said with his usual attitude, "they didn't offer me an outfit change when I died."

I jumped on that. "They? Who are *they*?"

"I was making a joke," Mal told me. "Really, I have no idea what happened. I don't remember dying. I just... woke up here and you couldn't see me."

"Like you told me in that dream," I said. God, that must've sucked.

"Yeah," Mal said.

As I stood there, looking at him, I felt tears well up in my eyes. "Oh, Mal," I said.

He backed away. "Please don't. It's already been upsetting enough without you crying again. Although thank you for doing the thing with the salt—and for the seven-hundred dollar e-book."

I half-sobbed, half-laughed at that. "Best seven-hundred dollars I ever spent."

He was embarrassed. "Yeah, well, I'm glad we're finally done with one-wind-is-yes, two-winds-are-no—Jesus was *that* frustrating."

As I stood there, looking at him, I knew that one of two terrible things was true. Either Mal had died and I was looking at his ghost, or I'd lost it and was having some kind of psychotic episode.

I cleared my throat, hoping against hope that I was going crazy—and Mal was really still alive and miles away from my house. "So... what do we do now?" I asked.

Mal looked at me. "I'm thinking that *you'll* want to start by getting dressed."

"Right," I said. "Shit. Right." I rushed over to grab a pair of running shorts from my clean laundry basket.

Mal pointed toward the front of my house. "FYI, your front door is still wide open because when it comes to strength, Pat-the-spirit-guide was not far off the mark. I am a sad little girl."

Malcolm

As Henry finally pulled on a pair of running shorts—thank God—I told him about all the weird rules of being dead. Like, everything was freaking heavy as fuck, and that before we'd triggered the binding spell, there'd been a force field that had kept me from touching him while he was awake.

I told him that I didn't sleep, that I wasn't hungry—although I was bitter about the whole no-cake thing.

Henry looked a little dazed as I followed him back to his entryway, where indeed his front door hung open.

And as he moved to close it, he must've seen someone out on the street, because he called out, "Hey!"

I squinted past him, and sure enough, dimly lit by the street lights, I could see a man—a very attractive man, in fact—getting out of his car. He'd parked in my spot—or at least it was the space on the street that I'd always thought of as *my spot*—right in front of Henry's house.

"Hello! Excuse me," Henry called, and the man stopped. As he looked back at us over the top of his car, his body language was wary.

And for good reason. It was extremely late—like last-call, bar-closing late. But the guy was alone, so maybe it was post-hookup-don't-wanna-stay-over-cause-no-thanks-this-won't-happen-again late.

The lateness of the hour meant *we* should've been wary, too, but Henry lowered his voice to say to me, "Let's see if he can see you!"

"Wait!" I said. Hadn't he been listening to my long list of new rules? "I'm not even sure I can leave your house!"

But Henry had opened the screen and was already halfway down the path to the street. Dressed only in those running shorts, he was moving swiftly but carefully due to his bare feet, which made him look both adorable and freaking hot. And yeah, I knew from the way the sexy guy on the street's body language shifted to *Why, hello there...* that he was gay, so...

I realized then that this man must be the oft-mentioned, new-to-the-'hood, Hot Neighbor Guy. And I wanted a closer look. Not to act on it in any way but, you know, it's not like I was dead—oh, wait.

I cautiously inched my way through the open screen, unwilling to get my ass zapped should there be some kind of real-estate-centric version of the force field.

But nothing bad happened.

So I went down the steps, and then hurried to catch up to Henry.

Hot Neighbor Guy had come around his car to meet him at the edge of the yard because of course he'd do that—*he* was neither blind nor dead.

"Sorry to bother you," Henry was saying in his incredibly charming way, "but, um... I had some friends over on Halloween, and one of them never made it home. I was wondering if you might've seen him getting into his car? It was parked here on the street."

Hot Neighbor Guy didn't look away from Henry as I approached, but see *Henry, dressed only in running shorts*, mentioned above. That didn't necessarily mean I was invisible to everyone but Henry.

I experimented by saying, "We're trying to create a timeline to help track him down."

And... Hot Neighbor Guy kept his piercing brown eyes glued to Henry. "Wow, that's... intense." Again, that could've just been one super-focused gay agenda.

Henry said, "He was wearing jeans and a green T-shirt. He's a little taller than me, very handsome, brown hair..."

"I'm not sure I'd say *very*, but thank you and hello, Hot Neighbor Guy, can you see me...?" I waved and then even clapped my hands directly in his face.

He didn't flinch. He didn't so much as blink as he smiled at H. "I definitely would've remembered seeing him. But no. Sorry."

I tried getting loud, to see if he could hear me. *"Can you hear me...?"*

"Whoa," he said. "It's suddenly... windy...?"

Henry turned and looked at me with real despair and disappointment in his eyes. *Shit.* I forced an *At least* you *can see and hear me, which is not nothing* apologetic smile.

Henry, however, looked like he was going to cry. He forced a smile that he aimed at Hot Neighbor Guy. "Okay," he said, backing away, "Sorry, yeah, thanks anyway."

He turned and headed back toward the house as I followed more slowly, still walking backwards. I couldn't help but notice that Hot stood there, watching Henry go with undisguised interest in his pretty eyes.

He was also not an idiot—he was telegraphing that interest quite clearly. And as Henry turned, waiting for me to follow him inside before closing his front door, Hot took the opportunity to wave to him. Henry, however, only waved back because he was polite.

"He seems... perfect," I pointed out.

But nope. Henry's complete lack of interest was very real and could not have been more pronounced.

"So now what do we do?" he asked, as if I were some sort of expert on being dead, but then answered his own question immediately. "Research. The *Crimson Book.*"

Oh.

Good...?

Henry

"When Pat was doing her thing," Malcolm said as he sat down next to me on the sofa, "she asked me why I was here."

I nodded. That was the first thing I'd searched for upon opening Pat's *Crimson Book,* after coming back inside. "This book says you're probably here because of some *powerful unfinished business.*"

I was hyper-aware of a lot of things as I flipped and skimmed through the e-book's literally endless pages. First and foremost was that Mal was now sitting next to me on the couch. The laptop was on my lap, and he had to lean in a bit to see the screen.

He seemed real enough in my peripheral vision.

But I didn't just see him—I felt him. His presence. A solid warmth.

I scrolled back to the page that discussed why a spirit might not immediately move on. And Mal leaned even closer to read it.

Neither one of us had mentioned my ill-timed kiss—or the fact that I was pretty sure that Mal had kissed me back in my dreams, which were maybe not really dreams after all...

But Mal had gotten to the part that indeed said, *Oftentimes, lingering spirits are found to have powerful unfinished business.*

"Yeah, but what?" Mal looked up to ask me. "There was nothing going on in my life. I mean, literally nothing is unfinished."

Well, he *was* much too young to die, and then there was his stuck-at-chapter-seven novel. But that was more abandoned than unfinished. Before I could bring that up, he was already reciting a list.

"I'm an only child, my parents are both gone—" he ticked his bullet-points off on his fingers "—I haven't been seeing anybody... I mean, I'm pretty sure I didn't stick around to copy-edit the thrilling follow-up to *America's Favorite Serial Killers.*"

I laughed at the ridiculousness of that book's extra-stupid title. It made me imagine a reality TV show where promising young serial killers competed for America's love and admiration, but then I stopped laughing as I realized that, speaking of serial-killing, we still didn't know how Mal had died. I mean, assuming he was really dead and I wasn't simply crazy...

"Do you think you were murdered?" I asked. "Maybe we have to catch your killer and bring them to justice."

Malcolm sat back on the sofa. He'd already told me he didn't remember how he'd died. But now he shrugged as he met my gaze. "I don't feel murdered."

I shook my head. "What does *murdered* feel like?"

"I guess... at least, I'd remember feeling scared...?" he answered slowly. "Or pissed off...? Instead, I'm just... here. But I've been thinking about it, and... I think the question to answer is why am I *specifically* here."

I didn't understand what he meant, so he kept going.

"In your house," Mal explained. "With you."

Of course the first thought that jumped into my head was about sex. The fact that, in all the years we'd known each other we'd never hooked up certainly made *my* business feel unfinished.

And the truth was, he certainly seemed to be here. I could see him, hear him and mostly importantly, I could touch him. And he could touch me. So why was he sitting way over there? Why weren't we already naked? I mean, if this was *my* fantasy—my private, personal episode of crazy—then he should be the complete Mal-of-my-dreams, right? The man who was not just funny and kind and smart and caring, but also sexy as hell...?

He'd been silent for a moment, so I glanced over and saw that he was watching me. He kind of smiled a little and took a deep breath—oh, God, here it came—and said, "I think my unfinished business is you."

Yes. Yes, it was. *Bow chicka bow bow...* I was a little tongue tied and feeling oddly shy, so all I managed to say was, "Me."

Mal nodded. "Yeah," he said. "You know, before, when we went outside...? I think I'm here to help you win your happily-ever-after with your perfect Hot Neighbor Guy."

That was so completely *not* what I'd expected him to say that I laughed. "Help me." What the hell did *that* mean?

He shifted on the couch, turning to face me eagerly as he continued. "Yeah. You know. Coach you through asking him out. Break the early-relationship ice. You suck at that."

I laughed again, in horror this time. "You're serious."

"You've always been a hopeless romantic. Maybe I'm still here to help you find your one true love." He *was* serious. He continued, "Hot Neighbor Guy is the complete package, including, you know, he's got a pulse..."

I was so shocked and dismayed, I launched myself off the couch and was all the way across the room before I stopped. There was no way I'd fantasize that Mal would say something like *that*. I kept my back to him so he couldn't see my face. "No," I said. "God. Mal, I don't want to. I'm not ready for... That's... *No.*"

"But you're never ready." His voice was gentle. "And unless you want me to spend eternity in purgatory or wherever the hell I am—with its no sleeping, no cake, not being able to lift things..."

I turned to look at him. "Of course I don't want that."

"Well, good." Mal stood up, too. "It's late. Those of us who still sleep need to sleep. We'll start planning *Project: Hot Neighbor Guy* first thing in the morning."

He made it sound like he was going to have fun with it—like it was some kind of game that we'd play together.

God, he was probably really dead—and he *still* didn't want me.

"Why am *I* standing?" Malcolm asked. "*You're* the one who has to go to bed.... Leave me the *Book*, and oh, set the computer screen to never-sleep…"

I adjusted the setting in a bit of fog, then left him there, reading.

I went to bed—hoping I'd wake up to find that this was all just a bad dream.

CHAPTER ELEVEN
Malcolm

An annoying thing about reading an e-book with infinity pages is that you're never more than one percent finished.

I spent the night reading many hundreds of pages, attempting to unlock the mystery of what, exactly, had happened to me—and what was to come—and the news was not good.

Also, using the computer's touch pad to turn the pages was impossible since my fingers were no longer human, so I had to get used to the actual physical right and left buttons on the keyboard. Pushing them was a total-concentration, exhausting full-body workout.

So yeah. That was *my* night. How was yours?

Henry's was uneventful.

I have to confess that, just before dawn, I wandered in his direction, and found he'd left his bedroom door open.

I stood there for a while, just watching him sleep.

And yeah, I know that's creepy, but I'm dead so fuck you. I was feeling appropriately sorry for myself, as well as mourning the loss of what might've been, so give me a break.

But it was finally morning—another bright, sunny SoCal day—and I was sitting in front of the computer when Henry finally emerged to eat his breakfast. Now he was back, dressed in running clothes.

"You sure you don't want to come?" he asked me.

I looked at him. "Very. I didn't like running when I was alive."

His mouth tightened, and I knew that he hated being reminded that I was dead. Still, he had to get used to it.

"All right," he said, heading out of the living room. "See you later."

"For your hot-neighbor-guy make-over!" I called after him. "We'll start by picking out what you're gonna wear, okay?"

"Yeah. Great." Henry turned back and smiled, but it was definitely forced—just like the super-psyched, extra-jolly tone I had added to my voice.

I watched him put in his earbuds and start up the music on his phone as he left the room, allowing myself to deflate only after I heard him open his front door and exit through the screen.

Jesus, this was gonna suck—helping Henry find true love with another man.

But the more of the *Crimson Book* that I'd read, the more I'd realized that it had to be done. Henry deserved a life filled with happiness, and I was gonna make sure he found it.

I turned my attention back to the book, but suddenly I was jerked up and off the sofa—as if there were an invisible rope around my waist.

I scrambled to stay on my feet even as I felt myself pulled forward—out of Henry's living room through the dining room doorway, out through the dining room toward the front of the house.

I slipped and slid and lost my balance as I fell into the entryway, scrambling to my feet only to slam face first into the edge of the wall beside the open front door. For a moment, I just stood there, my face mushed from this weird feeling of pressure and pulling.

"Gah!" I said. "What the fuck…?!"

I used all my feeble non-strength to slide toward the screen, and that released some of the pressure as I burst out of Henry's house like water from a geyser.

It was the weirdest fucking thing I've ever experienced or felt—and yeah, I know I've said that a lot recently. But this really did trump everything in my new, massive, post-death "weirdest fucking thing" file.

I was pulled through Henry's front yard, arms flailing as I worked to stay on my feet. Whatever was dragging me was clearly gonna drag me, even if I bumped along the ground, face-first. And I definitely didn't want *that* exciting new experience, thanks.

As I hit the street, I was yanked hard to the right, and I spotted Henry. He was running—about forty feet in front of me. Which is not *that* great a distance—like a couple of room lengths.

So I shouted. "Hey! *Hey! Henry!* HENRY!"

But he didn't stop or even turn around—no doubt he couldn't hear me over his music.

And he was running much too fast for me to catch him.

"Fuck!" I shouted. "*Fuuuhhhck!*"

Henry

I ran my regular loop around the neighborhood, keeping my pace on the slow side.

Mostly because I was dreading returning home to Mal's Hot Neighbor Guy make-over thing.

Jesus.

At least it was a beautiful day.

As I ended my run by hurdling some of the grasses and shrubs in my front yard, only stopping when I hit my front steps, I was aware of the peacefulness and serenity of my garden.

I was sweating—mostly because of the day's heat—I hadn't pushed myself *that* hard. But I checked my running app, then noticed that the front door's screen was open, which was weird.

I realized—holy crap—I'd been on auto-pilot when I'd left the house. No need to shut and lock the front door when Mal was home, except he wasn't home. Not really. Not invisible and inaudible to anyone who might walk through my open front door...

It was then—as I was imagining murderers and thieves just walking into my house—that someone put their hand, heavily, on my shoulder.

"No!" I shouted as I swiftly turned and slapped...

Malcolm...?

"Ow!" he said. He was indignant—and out of breath.

I pulled my earbuds out and shut off my music. "What are you doing out here?"

"Other than getting slapped?" he asked.

"You snuck up on me!"

"I wasn't sneaking," he shot back. "I was screaming the entire—" he grabbed my hand and turned it so he could see my phone—and the details on my running app "—two point five miles. All of Sherman Oaks is like, *Wow, windy day.*"

He stalked past me, through the open screen, into the house.

"But why did you follow me?" I asked, going inside, too, but then heading into the kitchen. I needed water, stat. "You said you didn't want to run."

As I grabbed a bottle of water and drank it, Mal sat down, right there on the kitchen floor. He was clearly exhausted—and shaken.

"I didn't exactly have a choice, Marathon Man," he said. "Right after you left, I got dragged along behind you."

Whoa, wait, what...? "You were *dragged*...?"

"Yup," Mal said. "I think that binding spell did a little bit more than make it possible for you to see me. After two point five miles of that hell, I can safely say that we've got—at most—a forty foot tether between us. So do me a huge-large and don't jump into your car and drive away, 'kay? God knows what'll happen to me. Although I've always wanted to fly..."

He was being flip, but I could tell that he was freaked out. I was, too. Terrified at his implication, I supported my suddenly shaky legs by leaning back against the counter. "I had no idea." I would never have run if I'd known.

It was clear that Mal knew that. I could also tell from the expression on his face that there was more bad news coming.

"It's possible I'm bound to your house, too," he said. "The farther away we ran, the more it felt like I was gonna... *dissolve* or... *evaporate*."

"Oh my God, are you okay?"

Malcolm nodded. "I feel much better now that we're back."

Better as in, less like he was going to *evaporate* or *dissolve*.

I had to do something besides stand there and think about Mal dissolving, so when I went to put my empty bottle in the recycling and saw that the container was full, I grabbed it and headed for the bin that sat out on the driveway, in front of the house.

Mal pushed himself to his feet so he could follow me outside. "But we should probably check the *Book*, make sure there's nothing else we missed. Like, your toenail clippings will now grow, overnight, into giant beanstalks."

I had to laugh at that, although my heart was still lurching. "God, I missed you," I told him, then dumped the recycling with a clatter, thinking, *Please don't ever dissolve.*

"Yeah, well," Mal said, "over the past few days, I've seen *way* too much of you. Quick, you've had clothes on for twenty whole minutes—it's time to get naked again!"

I laughed again, this time with embarrassment mixed in. "I *do* have to shower."

"Heads up!" Mal's voice sharpened as he turned toward the street. "Hot Neighbor Guy at four o'clock!"

Yup. There he was. My hot neighbor. He was dressed for work

in a very nicely fitting suit. He was standing near his car, watching me talk to myself and laugh wildly at nothing.

Great.

But he didn't seem too nonplussed by my crazy. In fact, he smiled and waved.

Now Mal was watching me as I stood there, staring back at Neighbor Guy, and I could tell he thought I was overcome by the hotness.

But no, that was just normal, freaked-out embarrassment that glued me to my driveway. I broke free, and bee-lined into the house.

"Why didn't you say something?" Mal asked as he chased me inside. "*Hey. Hi. How's it going? Good morning, I'm Henry.*"

"I was laughing like an idiot," I said, because I'd already given him a variation of *Really, Mal, I absolutely do not want to do this.* And that hadn't worked. Maybe if he thought that I was now mortified...

"Yes, you were," Mal agreed. "And *you* think you don't need my help. Hey, do you still do that weird cross-fit/gardening thing you used to do...?"

I did—every other day. And I probably would do it more often now that I couldn't run without the risk of Mal dissolving. But I just shook my head as I went into the bathroom, closing the door tightly behind me.

Even in life, Malcolm had been a through-the-bathroom-door shouter.

Now, he raised his voice to say, "Because I'm thinking *that's* what you should be doing out here, tomorrow morning when he leaves for work. And then you can casually stop, *Oh, hello. How are you? I'm Henry...* Of course we'll have to figure out what to tell him about your *missing friend*—" he added air quotes with his emphasis "—so he doesn't think you're a serial killer."

I sighed and turned on the shower, drowning out whatever else Malcolm might've said.

CHAPTER TWELVE
Henry

After I showered and dressed, I headed for the living room, prepared to have it out with Mal about his whole crazy Hot Neighbor Guy project.

There was no way I was doing this—allowing him to make me over so that I'd, what...? I wasn't even sure what the goal was. Get a date? Get laid? Get married and live happily ever after...?

That last one was no longer an option for me—it had died along with Mal.

As far as those other things...? Right now, I certainly didn't feel like dating or sleeping with *any*one, no matter how hot he allegedly was.

I braced myself for the confrontation, but when I stepped into the living room, Mal was standing over by the sliders, looking out into my back garden.

He didn't hear me come in. He was looking up at the sky and his face was pensive.

My laptop was open and the *Crimson Book* was on the screen. I stopped to see what part of the book Mal had been reading.

"*Goals and Desires of the Wandering Spirit.*" I read the page's heading aloud.

Mal glanced at me with the ghost of a smile, before turning back to the view out the window. "I never really appreciated clouds or how blue the sky is, back when I was alive," he said quietly. "But you always did."

"Photographer," I pointed out, even though my stomach churned at his *when I was alive*. I was still flipping back and forth between *I'm crazy* and *Mal's really dead*, but spending far more time on the second because why would I have a fantasy that left me so freaking unsatisfied?

"Exactly," Mal said. "You've always seen the beauty in everything and... All those times you tried to talk me into going up onto the roof to watch the sunset, back in school... God, I really regret saying no." He turned then, to face me. "You know it was because I was terrified of you, don't you?"

I had not known that. I shook my head, *no*, as Mal moved closer.

"Gina was right," he said. "About... what'd she call it? Our meet-cute. You were literally puking, but you were still the most... attractive, amazing person I'd ever met. The way you made me laugh... But you scared the hell out of me, so I just kept making all those excuses. I was a senior, you were too young. Then we were friends—don't want to screw *that* up. And I just pissed it all away and now... I'm dead."

God, this was everything I'd ever wanted to hear him say. Except for that last part. I took a step toward him. "Mal..."

But he held up his hands, saying, "No, just listen, okay?" and I stopped.

"I fucked up," Mal admitted as he moved past me toward the laptop, "because I was too afraid. But now you have this chance— this golden, shining, brand new chance with this beautiful, perfect man who's so completely into you... So let's do this. It's what I want for *you*. Now, go ahead and click play—" he was now next to my computer and he gestured down toward it "—so we can clarify exactly what I know you're gonna want for *me*."

I was confused. "Play...?"

Malcolm smiled. "For seven hundred dollars, you got bonus videos. Pat's got a lot to say about wandering spirits. Apparently that's what I am, so just... watch."

I met his eyes—he was so steady in his certainty. So I hit *play*, and a video clip started on my laptop screen.

There were absolutely no production values. It was just Pat, in all her magnificence, standing in front of a camera that had a pretty cheap microphone. Still, she exuded calm, and began by ringing some kind of chime.

"Wandering spirits," Pat said in her ghost-talking voice, which was probably also her YouTube-video and her community-theatre voice, "also known as wanderers or haunters, will be restless and in pain until their unfinished business is complete."

Aghast, I turned to Mal as she rang her chime again. "Are you in pain?"

He shook his head. "Shh, just..." He pointed to the computer where Pat was continuing her video lecture.

"Some wanderers have been in agony for centuries," she informed us. "Their pain has turned, understandably, to anger. A gentle approach—some kindness—will work in your favor as you consult with the experts who will help your spirit guests find the closure they need, to move on to a place of pleasure and peace."

She hit her chime again as the video ended.

"So... that's what *I* want," Mal told me. "To move on, ASAP, to that rockin' place of pleasure and peace. I'd really like to skip the whole centuries-of-agony thing. Okay?"

Oh, God. Yes, of course it was okay. I wanted him to skip that, too. I couldn't help myself—I reached out and hugged him, and he hugged me tightly back.

"I'll help you find closure," I whispered. Of course I would. Even if it meant...

"Thank you," Mal said, letting me go and stepping away. "Now... Let's go pick out your outfit, okay?"

I nodded, because yes, I would do this for him.

But no one said I had to like it.

Malcolm

Christ, I hated this.

I sat on H's bed as he modeled a pair of brightly colored running shorts and a tank top.

"No," I said. "Too slutty. Try the other shorts again."

Henry sighed. It was possible he hated this as much as I did. "But you already saw..."

"We need to get this right," I insisted.

I got another world-weary sigh as Henry stripped back down to his underwear.

Which is when the doorbell rang, several time in rapid succession.

Henry and I both turned—we could see the entryway through his open bedroom door—and before either of us could move, the door opened and Gina came barreling inside.

Carl was behind her—he, at least, looked sheepish about just waltzing on in.

"Henry...?" Gina called before she turned and saw us—or least she saw Henry—in the bedroom. At that point, she waltzed right in here, too. "Henry, you can't leave a message like *Malcolm's a ghost*, and then not answer your phone!"

"Gina," I said. "So good to see you respecting boundaries." I realized that both she and Carl were dressed in layers—to travel. To be fair, it was the fact that they were both rolling carry-on bags behind them that gave *that* away. Gina had left hers with Carl, who was still standing awkwardly by the front door—no doubt in part because Henry was still standing there in only his underwear.

Not that *that* would ever have stopped Gina.

"Sorry," Henry told her, waving *hello* to Carl, "I went out for a run and then I had to shower..."

"And then you were avoiding me," Gina finished his sentence for him, hands on her hips. "Don't deny it!"

Henry sighed. "Why don't we sit down and—"

"No," Gina said. "We have to get to LAX. Remember? That job in Japan I was so excited about...?"

"Oh. Yeah. Right," Henry said. He looked out at Carl. "You're going, too?"

Gina didn't let Carl answer. "He's my first AD, and yeah. *Bad* time for drama!"

"Sorry," I said.

Henry glanced at me before telling Gina, "Malcolm says he's sorry—that he *died*."

Gina gasped. "You see him? Right now!" She turned to tell Carl, "Oh my God! This is worse than I thought!" She turned back to glare at Henry. "We took a Lyft over here. You need to put some clothes on and drive us to the airport while we talk about this."

Carl cleared his throat from the entryway. "Yeah, I'm not sure I'm eager to get into a motor vehicle driven by a man who has an invisible friend."

"He's not insane," Gina argued in Henry's defense, "he's having a mental breakdown!"

Carl looked from Gina to Henry and back. "And that's better how...?"

Henry spoke up. "I'm sorry, no, I can't leave the house. Malcolm might... dissolve."

I sighed. "You gotta admit that sounds slightly less than sane," I said to Henry.

"But it's true," Henry told me.

Gina gasped again. "Are you talking to him?" Again, she turned to tell Carl, "He's talking to him!"

Carl already had his phone out. "And we... are... getting another Lyft..." he said as he scrolled through the app, "to LAX... right... *now*. Oh, good, there's one nearby."

Gina, meanwhile was looking at Henry and now she reached out and took both of his hands. "Henry." She was sincere, but that didn't make her less annoying. "Malcolm's not dead. He's just a fucking coward who ran away after you kissed him, and now you're freaking out. You really wanted this, badly, and now you're hallucinating, obviously."

"Obviously," I said.

Henry looked at me in exasperation before turning back to Gina. "Gina..."

She cut him off. "And you've always been a *little* bit agoraphobic so I'm not completely surprised that *Malcolm*—" she used exaggerated air quotes "—will *dissolve* if you leave the house."

"I'm not..." Henry started to argue about her agoraphobia accusation, but then clearly decided not to fight her—good call. Instead he asked, "When do you get back?"

"Late on Wednesday," she said. "A little before midnight."

"Oh, good," Henry said. "Pat's coming over at four AM on Thursday, if I haven't helped Mal move on by then—"

"Pat?" Gina blinked at Henry so hard, I thought for a moment she'd thrown a clot. "The spirit guide? The one who came over, and then you screamed at me over the phone because this was all just some mean joke that I was supposedly helping Malcolm play on you...? Is that the Pat who's coming over on Thursday at four fucking AM...?"

Henry winced. It was obvious that he felt bad about that. "Yeah, sorry, that was before Mal convinced me he was here, and we did the binding spell..."

"Oh, my God. *Binding* spell...?"

Carl spoke up from the entryway. "This is why we're getting a Lyft."

Henry turned to me. "It shouldn't be *that* hard to prove you're really here."

"Oh!" I said. "I once read a story where there was this ghost and there was only one person—his great-grandson—who could see him and..."

Gina snapped her fingers in front of Henry's face. To her, he was gazing into space, listening to silence. "Henry."

He gave her the hand. "Hang on, Mal's telling me something."

"So the great-grandson used a book," I continued, enjoying Gina's discomfort perhaps a tad too much, "to prove to his girlfriend that his grandfather's ghost was—"

"Lyft's here," Carl intoned. "Henry. It was nice to see you, although I didn't expect to see quite this much."

Henry looked down—yes, he was still wearing only his underwear. "Oh," he said.

"Henry," Gina said, "We have to go. If you really can't drive us to the airport..."

Henry made an apologetic face. "I'm sorry, I really can't."

Gina nodded. "I'll email you from Tokyo. And, listen, I know that Mal's not dead because he just blocked me from texting him."

Now it was Henry's turn to gasp as he told me, "Someone's using your phone."

"Oh, my God!" Gina said.

Carl opened the front door. "Gina, tick tock..."

Gina hugged Henry fiercely.

"Answer me when I email you," she ordered him, then stepped back, holding his head so that he was forced to look into her eyes. "Promise?"

Henry nodded.

"Say it!" Gina demanded.

With a sigh of long suffering, Henry said, "I promise I will answer your email."

"Thank you," Gina said. She took a deep breath and exhaled it hard. "You're gonna get through this," she told him. "We'll get you the help you need."

And with that, she pulled her rolling bag out of the house, following Carl. At least they had the manners to close the door behind them.

Henry turned to look at me.

"You are really here, right?" he asked.

I leaned forward and shouted in his face. "*YEEEEEESSS!*"

As Henry got blasted by the wind noise, he closed his eyes and stepped back until I stopped.

"All righty then," he finally said in the blessed silence.

"See how exhausting that is?" I told him. "Come on, let's finish picking out the perfect clothes to launch your happily-ever-after with Hot Neighbor Guy.

CHAPTER THIRTEEN
Henry

After Gina and Carl left for the airport, the next few hours—my official make-over—were kinda fun. *If* I didn't think too hard about why Mal and I were doing this, or the fact that Mal was no longer a living, breathing human being...

I put on one of my studio photo-shoot playlists—music was a good way to set the mood. And since Mal kept making *This is fun, isn't it* noises, I decided to embrace that—to go all in.

I didn't know how long Mal would be present in my life before he moved on to the mysterious spirit world, as it was called in the *Crimson Book*. From what I'd read, the length of time he would stick around seemed a toss-up between *forever* and *temporarily*. The book didn't say it outright, but the subtext dripped with a heavy serving of Carl's ominous *tick-tock*. Like, we really needed to expedite Mal's departure ASAP, because the longer he lingered in the world-of-the-living, the greater the odds that he'd wind up stuck here for eternity.

And as much as I wanted him to stay with me, his *forever* in this world was filled—as he was fond of reminding me—with no-cake.

But here and now, Mal was delighted with my choice of music. "A good make-over montage needs the right soundtrack," he said.

So we both danced a little as I once again went through the wardrobe options for tomorrow morning—the planned time for me to "run into" Hot Neighbor Guy again.

Of course we argued about that—especially when Malcolm called tomorrow's planned encounter a *meet-cute*.

"I've already met him," I reminded him. "When we were checking if he could see you...?"

"That doesn't count," Mal said, shaking his head *no* at the shorts and tank that he'd made me put on again, even though we'd both already rejected it.

"How can it not count?" I asked as I changed into outfit number two—black shorts and a faded sky-blue T-shirt that was fraying at the collar and was just *slightly* too tight. "I had a conversation with the guy in my front yard at Sweet-Jesus-o'clock in the morning. He was probably drunk, I was definitely wild-eyed..."

"And barely dressed," he pointed out. "*But*... you still don't know his name, and he doesn't know yours, so it's not official."

"So wait, you're saying formal introductions make it official...?" I shot him a *that's ridiculous* look. "I don't think it works that way. I think you meet, and it's cute or it's not."

"Okay, then it was already cute, but now we need to make it even cuter," Mal said. "A re-meet-cut*er*." He leaned on the last syllable of *cuter* as he made the motion for me to turn in a circle, which I obediently did.

"This is the one," he decided. "It's effortlessly sexy. Casually hot. *This* is what you wear. Now, we do your hair."

"My *hair*...?" I asked. "What's wrong with my hair?"

"Nothing," he said in a tone that implied *everything*. "I just want to consider the options."

"Like, leave it on my head or shave it off?" I asked.

"If those are your only two choices," he chided. "Well, no wonder..."

So yeah, we went into the bathroom and now I stood in front of *that* mirror as I wet my hair and combed it straight back—like a 1920s silent film star—as Mal tried not to laugh.

Yeah, that was a hard *nope* for me, too.

Next I tried mousse—I rarely used much of any kind of product—but even a small handful of the foamy stuff made my hair stand up straight all over my head. The look was a mix of Albert Einstein, Bozo-the-clown, and a guy who just put his finger in a light socket.

Mal pretended to consider it, again making the *Spin so I can see it from all angles* motion with his finger.

I gave him another finger entirely, then went to work taming it—and turning it into a slightly more polished version of my usual messy look.

That got a big, nodded *yes* from my judging-panel-of-one.

I thought that meant we were done—in fact, my playlist was on the verge of ending—but no.

"Now we work on body language," Mal told me, leading the way into my living room, because we needed space to... what...?

Stretch in prep...?

"Okay," Mal continued. "Before we get to the actual scenario—you're outside working out and oh, look, here comes Hot Neighbor Guy—let's go over a few basics, starting with eye contact."

I sighed and raised my hand. "Gay man," I reminded him. "I know all about eye contact."

"Do you, H?" he asked. "Do you really? Because you spend a lot of time looking *not* at other people. And whenever you can—which is pretty damn frequently—you hide behind your camera lens."

He was right. But part of my problem was that there was really only one person with whom I wanted to have long, extended eye contact. And I looked into his eyes right then. "This better?" I asked.

Mal cleared his throat. "Yeah, but you know, blink every now and then or it's weird."

I laughed. "I blink."

"I know," he said, laughing, too. "I'm just being an asshole. And see...? There you go—that little what-the-fuck smile...? That, plus the eye contact...? That's... very hot. I approve."

"Oh, thank God," I said with an eye roll of epic proportions, and he laughed again.

"Moving on to presentation," Mal said.

"This should be good," I said, "and please don't instruct me on the proper way to tie a bow around my dick."

He laughed again at that. "Having seen you naked, there's no need to accessorize that... particular feature."

Okay, now I was a little embarrassed, thinking about all the time I'd spent naked while Mal was invisible and trapped in my house.

But my nakedness had clearly had little impact on him. "I'm talking about *this* kind of presentation," he said, gesturing to himself.

I realized he was leaning against my bar table. I'd seen him standing exactly that same way, many times before—down to the little smile that played about his graceful lips. It always made me think of that expression, *A tall drink of water.* He looked deliciously cool and refreshing.

I looked more closely and saw that Mal's left elbow was against the table, which made the muscles in that arm pop enticingly against his T-shirt sleeve. It also made his shirt stretch—just slightly across his broad shoulders and his well-defined chest. His hands rested at the top of his jeans, his thumbs in his waistband, his fingers loosely locked. It pulled my attention down to the front of his well-fitting, faded jeans—not by accident, I realized. His legs were long and strong and went on kinda forever, with his feet casually crossed at the ankles.

"Ah," I said.

"Right?" he agreed. "Now, you do it."

I looked down at myself, standing the way I usually stood—both feet securely planted, weight balanced and steady. This was how I stood when I took a photograph, or—as Mal would put it—when I *hid behind my camera lens.*

I leaned my weight over to my right side, hip slightly out, which immediately made me feel off-kilter and awkward. What was I supposed to do now with my left leg? Just let it flap? I used it instead as a kind of ballast, resting the ball of my left foot slightly on the floor, left knee casually bent. I put my right hand on my right hip, which somehow helped me to not fall over, but that left my left arm flapping uselessly around. I toyed with putting my left hand on my left hip, but that felt far too Super-Girl. And it wasn't possible to cross one arm, so I ended up reaching up and resting my aimless left hand on my right shoulder.

Mal laughed. "Oh, my God," he said. "Please tell me you're kidding."

"This is stupid. This isn't me." Crossly, I resumed my usual balanced stance.

"*This,*" he told me, imitating me by putting his left hand onto his right shoulder, "is so tightly wound and closed off, it's a wonder that even *I* haven't run screaming from the house."

"I was being casual," I tried to explain. "Also…? If you do, you'll dissolve."

"Look." Mal folded his arms across his chest—which made the muscles in *both* his arms pop. "Don't come close," he said, then opened his arms widely into a welcoming gesture. "Come close." He did it again, folding his arms. "Don't come close…" Open arms. "You see how this works?"

I sighed.

"And you were right," he said. "This isn't you. Part of your charm is your WYSIWYG (pronounced: whizzy-wig) presentation. So let's skip ahead. Let's say you're on your date with Hot Neighbor Guy, and there's lots of eye contact, and its time to find out if there's a similar spark when you kiss. So... what do you do?" *Wait twelve years to see if maybe he was ever gonna get around to kissing me...?* Things I didn't say aloud. Instead, I said, "This is where I might need a little help."

Mal nodded as if he knew just how hard that was for me to admit. He didn't tease me, which was nice. "You start by touching. You could go for his hand, which'll tell you a lot, right away, because hand-holding is inherently romantic. But that also means it's fraught with peril. No one wants to be pulled-away from. So if you want to make that first touch less scary, and more, you know, friendly, you should go for the shoulder."

He demonstrated, putting his left hand on my right shoulder. And he was right, the gesture was definitely friendly. His hand felt warm against my T-shirt—how could he be warm if he was dead? Maybe it was an illusion or a by-product of the binding spell.

"So if you do this, and he doesn't back away," Mal continued, "you can move your hand like this." He brought his hand up to the back of my neck—and no, it wasn't an illusion. His hand *was* warm against my bare skin. "And move in closer. Look at his mouth. If he looks at yours...? You kiss him."

He moved tantalizingly close, and yeah, I was definitely looking at his mouth. But he abruptly let me go and took a few steps back.

"Or..." I suggested after clearing my throat a few times. "I could just ask: *May I kiss you?*"

"You could," Mal agreed. "Spoken consent is always great. But it's not always romantic. I mean, it *can* be but... And you *do* get consent from that eye contact. And by making sure that your touch is possessive, but not so much that he can't pull away."

I nodded. *He.* Meaning Hot Neighbor Guy. Jesus, I hated this.

"Moving on," Mal clapped his hands together. "Okay, I'll be Hot Neighbor Guy. I'm heading to work, and I go to my car and you're out in your front yard doing burpees."

Really...?

"Go on," Mal commanded. "Do burpees."

I sighed and began doing burpees—squatting, then pushing my feet out and back into a plank, then back to a squat, and jumping, arms up, into the air. Rinse and repeat.

"Well, *I'd* definitely notice that," Mal said. "But in case I don't, *you* see *me* and next time you're up on your feet, you wave to me. Go on. Wave to me."

This time I went from the squat to a wave and I'll admit that it might've been a bit tentative.

"*That's* how you're going to wave?" Mal asked.

It wasn't *that* awful of a wave. "Is there a better way...?" I asked.

"Yeah," Malcolm told me. "Look in a mirror. Wave like the guy you see in the reflection. You're hotter than Hot Guy. Wave like this..."

Mal lifted his chin in a nod of recognition, then pointed and waved, as a smile broadened on his handsome face. "Huh?" he said. "Huh? See what I'm doing?"

I tried. The head thing was too weird, so I simply did a basic point into a hopefully less-awful wave.

But Mal laughed. "It's not *Mommy, the lion escaped from his cage...!*" He pointed, arm outstretched straight in front of him, as if in sheer terror. "Into *Excuse me, Mrs. Twimbly? May I have the pass to the boy's room?*" He made his so-called wave look more like a timidly raised hand, his shoulders up around his ears.

I laughed a mix of my outrage, dismay, and amusement. "That's not what I did."

Mal laughed, too, in more pure amusement. No doubt about it— he was having fun with this, the way he did with practically everything. Being dead wasn't slowing him down. "That's *totally* what you did. It should be *Hey! You!*" He pointed again, and I saw that his finger was aimed much higher than mine had been. More like an *Oh, Waiter, we'd like more wine!* than an accusatory answer to *Do you see the killer, here in the courtroom?* He continued, "*Looking good, Hot Neighbor Guy!*" He tossed off his wave. It was more like a free-floating salute than my mix of, yes, half-heartedly raising my hand plus semi-pope-wave. He kept going, "*And yes*, I *am looking good, too!*"

Yes, again, he *was* looking good. Mal always looked good.

He turned and ordered me, "Do it."

I imitated him.

And even though my *oh-waiter* point was a little too *Saturday Night Fever* inspired, and my wave a bit too Marine Corps, Mal nodded his approval.

"Much better," he said. "Okay, so I'm heading for my car, but don't wait for me to come to you. Walk toward me—" again, he demonstrated "—with that same King-of-the-World attitude, and say

Hey! I'm Henry. I'm sorry I didn't introduce myself the other night—oh, by the way, my missing friend turned up. He's okay."

Mal stood there, holding out his hand for me to shake.

I took it, unhappy with what he'd just said. "But you're not okay."

Mal tightened his grip on my hand, pulling me toward him, hard—it was the giant-asshole-pull-shake favored by the current traitor-in-chief, and it nearly knocked me off my feet.

"But I will be okay," Mal told me, "if you do this right." He released me. "Okay, so he goes, *I'm glad to hear that. I'm Jizzy McMasturbater.*"

"You want me to spend the rest of my life with someone named *Jizzy McMasturbater...?*"

"Yeah," Mal said. "And you're welcome, because now, no matter *what* his real name is—Irving Fartington or Bob Knob—it won't be as terrible as Jizzy McMasturbater."

"Thanks...?" I said, laughing despite myself. Mal's brain really was an amazing place.

"Moving on, *you* say, *Nice to meet you, Jizzy.*" Now he was being me, pitching his voice slightly higher so that he sounded younger—but I wasn't *that* much younger than he was. *"Hey, I was wondering if you want to go out, grab some dinner, maybe tonight?"*

"But I can't go out," I pointed out, citing the forty-foot rule. If I went out to dinner with Hot Neighbor Guy... "You'll dissolve."

"Oh, shit, yeah." Mal had forgotten about that. He quickly re-grouped, again, giving me a new line-reading: *"Hey, Jizzy, I was wondering if you want to come over to my place for dinner tonight. Aaand... that's* a little weirdly intimate for a first date, but we can work with it. Especially if you say *I grill a mean steak,* which is true." He looked at me hard. "Are you remembering all this? Do you need to write it down?"

I crossed my arms—closed body language, I know, I know—because, come on.

"Hi, Jizzy," I said, my tone heavy with attitude, *"my best friend's a ghost who wants us to fall in love. Wanna come over to my place for dinner? Hashtag Steak."*

Mal crossed his arms, too. "Go on, mock the dead guy. But take it from the top and do it right. Walk toward me."

I hesitated. "Like you just did...?"

Malcolm rolled his eyes. "No. Walk like an ostrich. Yes! Walk like I just did."

Now I was completely in my head about walking. Should I swing my arms or not...?

"You know, maybe you *should* try walking like an ostrich." Mal demonstrated, lifting his knees and bobbing his head—hands under his arms, like the wings of a giant bird.

I laughed—and he did, too. His laugh was infectious, and suddenly I was able to walk again. Maybe not as King-of-the-World-y as Mal, but enough to merit a high-five and a shoulder-shake.

I remembered what he'd said about touching, and I couldn't help it—I looked at his mouth, and I swear to God he looked at mine, too. And for a half a second, I was certain that he was going to kiss me.

And just as I was thinking that *I* should do it—I should kiss *him*—he backed away.

"By George, I think he's got it!" he said with a perfect 'Enry 'Iggins accent that successfully broke whatever mood or moment that had been.

Even worse, we were not done here.

"Take it again from the top," Mal commanded, and we started the whole damn thing, all over again, from the pointing and the wave.

CHAPTER FOURTEEN
Malcolm

Henry left both Netflix and the TV on for me, and as he slept, I glommed seven straight hours of *Sense8*, which he'd always tried to get me to watch back when I was still alive.

I'd never had time.

I immediately knew why he'd loved it—the characters and story were great, yes, but the locations and photography were insanely beautiful.

But now Henry had been up for about an hour and it was time to head outside for this morning's carefully choreographed collision with Hot Neighbor Guy—also known as That Lucky Bastard.

I'd been following H around for a while, clapping my hands at him and saying things like, "It's time to get dressed!" and "Time to brush your teeth!" and "Don't forget to fix your hair!"

Now, my message was, "Let's do this thing!"

Henry had never been much of a morning person, but today he was dragging harder than usual. Still, he opened his front door and held the screen for me as we emerged into the fresh, cool, still-early morning.

Hot Neighbor Guy's car was parked in *my* spot—right out front. I wasn't sure which house he lived in, but as I scanned the neighbors' yards, there was no sign of movement.

Henry sighed and said, "I've been thinking about this."

I narrowed my eyes at him. "Don't think. Just stick to the plan. Start your workout, I'll watch for him and shout when he's coming."

But Henry just stood there as he sighed again. "Malcolm, this is... crazy."

Oh my God, Hot Neighbor Guy had appeared out of nowhere—but probably from the detached garage apartment of the house directly across the road. "Get ready," I announced. "Here he comes!"

Henry went into a sprint—good choice, because he could run

impressively fast. But he was going in the wrong direction—instead of heading for the street, he'd bolted back toward me, and I realized that he was attempting to escape around the far side of the house.

"What are you doing?" I stepped in front of him, and he screeched to a stop. "Where are you going?"

Henry was wild-eyed. "This is a mistake!" He feinted to the right and I foolishly moved with him—and he went around me the other way.

"God damn it," I said. "I'm gonna regret this."

I grabbed him by the T-shirt and, harnessing all of my pitiful strength, I somehow managed to fling him back around and down, toward the center of the front yard, mere feet from where Hot Neighbor Guy was now approaching his parked car.

Henry tripped over a clump of his exquisite drought-resistant tall grass and skidded to an ungraceful landing in a patch of mulch.

"*Ow!*" I shouted, too. Thanks to the binding spell, I also hit the ground, feeling every unfortunate bounce.

Just as I'd hoped, Hot Neighbor Guy saw Henry fall, and he rushed over to help.

"Oh, my God," he said in his perfect voice through his perfect mouth, "are you okay?"

Telling Henry not to think was probably a mistake, because he certainly wasn't thinking as he jabbed the air in my direction. "That asshole just pushed me!"

"Asshole?" Hot echoed, his perfect forehead wrinkled with his puzzlement.

"He can't see me, Mr. Rude," I reminded Henry.

"Oh God!" he said. "Right. Yes. It was, um… this *rock*. This *asshole* rock."

A man as cute as Henry—with those big blue eyes and that ass—could get away with being charmingly quirky or, let's face it, even downright weird. However, he'd left both of those in the rearview mirror during his last odd encounter when he'd shared a hilarious joke with his recycling bin.

Hot put a little more distance between them—just a smidge, but…

"And… we're losing him," I said. "Say something!"

"I don't know what to say," Henry answered me, which was worse than saying nothing.

"I'm sorry…?" Hot asked.

I saw the flash of panic cross Henry's face, and I knew he was nanoseconds away from abandoning *Project: Hot Neighbor Guy* and running for the house.

"Please," I begged. "Please, don't blow this! I really don't want to be in agony for centuries!"

Henry gulped as he shot me a look of total anguish, but then he did it. He rallied. "I don't know what to say... other than, thank you for coming to my rescue."

That was a damn fine save. And Hot's perfect face relaxed into a perfect smile. "No worries," he said as he held out a hand and helped Henry back to his feet.

And then, there they were, with Hot still clasping Henry's hand, as if they were greeting each other with a gentlemanly shake.

I could almost see Henry's brain stutter and short as he moved to the post-handshake point in the script we'd worked on so rigorously.

"Nice to meet you—" Henry started, and I cut him off.

"Don't call him Jizzy!" I said. "*I'm Henry.*"

Henry nodded. "I'm Henry Collins," he said.

Hot's smile was warm as he kept his hold on Henry's hand. "Rick Baker."

"See?" I told Henry. "Before Jizzy you might've thought Rick Baker was a little basic as far as names go. Now it's delightfully normal."

"Nice to finally meet you," Rick said as he also finally released Henry's hand. "Your friend ever turn up?"

"Yes!" Henry jumped, no doubt startled at how easy it was going to be to tick *Not a Serial Killer* off Rick's list. "Yes. He's, um... He's okay."

Not a lie because even though I was dead, I could've been far less okay.

"Time to bring it home," I told Henry as I gave him yet another push, this time directly in Hot Rick's direction.

From Rick's perspective, Henry had suddenly tripped again.

"Whoa, there!" Rick said, and like any good Prince Charming, he deftly caught Henry and kept him from hitting the ground.

They now were in a full-body embrace, and I should've been celebrating, because together we'd just created one very nice re-meet-cuter that would hold up in the years to come.

It was love at first sight, I could imagine a ten-years-older Rick saying as he twinkled his eyes fondly at Henry. *I spent days trying to get up the nerve to meet him. And then—I am such a lucky man—he just fell into my arms...*

I should've been celebrating our success, but instead I was battling a weird wave of jealousy—that Rick was alive and I wasn't. That Rick was smiling as he gazed into Henry's eyes, before dropping his focus to Henry's extremely kissable mouth...

But Henry had, apparently, forgotten everything I'd taught him, because he was not looking back at Rick with that sexy smolder I knew he could deliver. Instead he'd gone into a full babble.

"Sorry!" Henry told Rick. "Sorry! I, um, tried a new protein shake and I...guess it isn't quite enough before a heavy-duty workout."

And okay. Maybe it had started as a babble, but it had found solid legs.

I forced a smile. "Amazing save!" I told Henry. "You're getting really good at this!"

I could tell he desperately needed me to celebrate his victory, so I triumphantly ostrich-walked around them in a circle. And that made Henry laugh.

And yeah, Hot Rick was captivated by Henry's smile.

But Henry gently disengaged himself from Rick's grasp as he told me, "Thank you."

"You're welcome." Rick and I, both, said it in a near-perfect unison.

"He's totally into you," I added.

"Hey look," Rick said. "I gotta get to work, but do you wanna have dinner sometime?"

Henry looked startled—as if he'd forgotten that that was the entire point of this charade. "Um..."

Um...? What the fuck was *Um...?* "Say yes!" I demanded, reminding him of the plan. "Steak! Here! Tonight!"

Henry cleared his throat. "How about you, um, come over tonight," he asked awkwardly, "let me cook you a steak...?"

Hot Rick's smile was a strong clue that he found nothing awkward or too-intimate about a dinner-at-home invitation as a first date.

So Henry kept going. "Around seven...?"

"That sounds great," Rick said. "See you tonight."

And with that, Rick Baker, formerly known as Hot Neighbor Guy, walked over to his car, got in, and drove his perfect, not-dead ass away.

CHAPTER FIFTEEN
Henry

I spent the rest of the day in a funk.

Mal went back to watching Netflix as I attempted to finish up the work on the Gorfney wedding photos.

It pissed me off that he was so freaking okay with my dinner date with Rick Baker. But every time I made up my mind to go and talk to him about it, I stopped because I remembered how desperately he wanted to move on.

He was working to avoid centuries of pain.

I was avoiding my phone—and potential messages from morgues and hospitals—and just generally being a whiney baby-man with no empathy to spare for my dead best friend.

So... The day slowly ticked by, and I didn't bring it up.

I just defrosted some really nice steaks that I'd been saving in my freezer for...

For Mal. Okay? For a night when he was going to be here for dinner. I'd bought them because I knew that he'd both love and appreciate what he'd always called my *grilling prowess*. Like that was a real thing.

But now he couldn't eat—he no longer got hungry because he was dead—and he stayed on the sofa while I grilled the steaks for my dinner with Rick Baker.

By 6:55, I was showered and dressed in a button down shirt with my best pair of jeans. The table was set, candles were lit, the food was cooked—I had a set of plate warmers that really worked to keep the meal piping hot.

I did one last survey of the room—no dust bunnies in sight—as Mal sat down at the end of the table. He was upbeat and smiling and so fucking cheerful that if he hadn't already been dead, I might've killed him.

"Rick seems terrific," Mal said, then laughed a little. "He's certainly not afraid of diving headfirst into a relationship."

Like *some* people I knew... Still, I contained my snark. I knew despite his upbeat attitude that he had to be at least a *little* unsettled. "Are you nervous?" I asked.

He looked both surprised and confused. "About... Rick?" he asked.

"About moving on," I said. About *Rick*...? Was he serious...?

"Oh," Mal said. "I... I don't know what I feel. I'm... not sure when it'll happen. Maybe when you kiss him. Maybe when you..." He cleared his throat.

Holy fuck. I stared at him. "You want me to *sleep* with him...? Tonight?"

"Well, probably not tonight," he said. "Because you're you and, well... But, sex is part of falling in love, so... *Want* isn't quite the right verb, but... yeah. Yes. That's a big part of what I want for you—what I've always wanted for you. For you to find. Your Mr. Right, you know?"

I shook my head. If there was ever a time to speak, it was now. *You're my Mr. Right...*

But Mal, of course, wasn't done. "But I don't know how any of this works. For me to move on. It might have to be..." He searched for the word. "Glorious."

"Mal," I whispered back. "I'm gonna do whatever you need me to do. I'm just not sure I can do it... *gloriously*."

He nodded and made an attempt to smile. "Thank you. Really. And in case it happens fast and I don't get to say goodbye, you need to know that I'm *so* grateful. Both that you were my best friend for all these years and—"

Oh my fucking God, I hated this.

"I do know," I told him as I took one step and then another, toward him. "I want you to find peace. I do. I just wish..."

Mal stood up, and for one crazy second I was sure he was going to run out of the room. But instead, he stood his ground. "Don't say it," he whispered, then begged me, "Please."

"If this is goodbye..." I looked into his eyes. "I get to say whatever I want. I also get to do this."

I put my hand on his shoulder—just as he'd taught me. And when he didn't pull away, I moved my hand to the back of his neck. Skin against skin.

I knew Mal was dead and what I was touching wasn't his body but rather his binding-spell conjured spirit, but he was warm to my touch. Heat also flared in his eyes. It was all that I needed to know, and I leaned in and up to kiss him.

His lips—his mouth—were so soft and sweet. My heart pounded and my thoughts tornadoed as the entire world fell away.

So I deepened the kiss—and he opened for me—my tongue against his...

It was the way I should've kissed him twelve fucking years ago, and we both knew it.

But then he pulled back, and of course I released him as I said the words. I mean, I had to. How could I not? "I love you."

Mal closed his eyes briefly as he shook his head. "I'm dead, so it's *loved*. With a D on the end," he whispered. "Past tense."

And he needed to move on... I knew that, but...

The doorbell rang before I could say anything, as we both just stood there, fighting our tears.

Mal won that fight, smiling and even doing excited jazz-hands as he said, "Showtime!"

So I wiped my eyes and went to open the door.

Malcolm

That fucking kiss.

It damn near wrecked me.

Henry loved me.

Hearing that, feeling that, knowing the truth...

It was a full-on miracle that I managed to stay upright afterward—that I wasn't in a crumpled, sobbing heap on the floor.

I'd made a lot of noise about the lack of cake here in the afterlife. But the real truth was that I regretted *this*—the fact that I'd never taken the risk to let Henry love me—so much more.

I sagged a bit in my misery as he left the dining room and went to answer the door.

"Hi. Rick. Come on in." Henry's voice was subdued.

But the wall held me up, and by the time he brought Rick back, I'd successfully returned to cheerleader mode.

Rick had changed out of his business suit, but had dressed for the occasion in a nice pair of snugly-fitting jeans and the kind of shirt you'd wear to look extra-good on a first date. He was also wearing the type of hat that only a really handsome man could pull off—in the house…? And yes, I'd definitely edited too many books set in the 1960s and 70s, because that bugged me a little. Take off your freaking hat while you're inside, Rick…

"Your house is adorable," he told Henry as he looked around.

"Thanks." Henry was still visibly shaken, but Rick didn't seem to notice that.

"Normally I hate hats," I said, hoping a little tempered snark might help return Henry's tilting world to normal, "but he pulls it off. That's a rare skill."

But Henry just shook his head at me, as Rick stepped closer to examine first one then another and another of Henry's framed photographs.

"Hmmm," he said.

"And, look, he likes your photos," I pointed out.

Henry's body language was sharply *Let's get this over with*, as he took the warming covers off the dinner plates.

But Rick only saw the food. "Oh, man, that looks fantastic. I'm so hungry. Can we…?"

"Please! Yes! Sit," Henry picked up one of the bottles that he'd opened for the meal. "Would you like some wine?"

"Ooh," Rick said, making a face as he sat and opened his napkin with an extremely foodie flap, "I'm very picky." But he gestured for Henry to show him the labels.

Henry held out both bottles—one red, one white.

Rick damn near recoiled in his horror. "Oh, no. Never white. Never."

I'm not a wine drinker, but *really*…?

I swear I didn't say a word, but I must've exhaled a little loudly, because Henry glanced at me as Rick examined the label on the bottle of red.

Rick made an *Ew* face, but he poured himself a glass. "My motto's usually *Life's too short to drink shitty wine*," he announced, "but tonight the excellent company more than makes up for it."

"Okay," I said, in hopes of reassuring both Henry and my own self, "*that* was both douchey and charming, but he's a wine guy, so that explains the douchey. And no one's perfect—if he were perfect that would be unsettling."

Henry shot me an exasperated look as Rick smiled and lifted his wineglass in a toast.

"Here's to the start of a beautiful, new friendship," he said.

Henry clinked his glass to Rick's, but his smile was definitely forced.

Henry

Rick was a bit like Malcolm—they both loved to talk. But Mal liked to talk because he loved language and words and storytelling and descriptions.

Rick liked the sound of his own voice.

To be fair, he had a very nice voice.

I was also appreciative of not having to do a lot of heavy conversational lifting as Rick intoned and expounded his way through our entire dinner.

I'm sure the steaks were good—I'd cooked them perfectly. But I didn't taste much of anything and I sat there, listening to Rick and trying not to stare at Mal, to burn his image into my brain.

I didn't want him to leave, and I found myself thinking, *What if he stayed...?*

Life would be strange—Gina would hate it. I'd become the eccentric old photographer with the invisible boyfriend.

Then I found myself thinking about kissing Mal—and the way he'd kissed me back. He'd stopped kissing me, that was true, but before he'd stopped, he *had* kissed me back. And *that* had been unbelievably great...

Except he'd told me, quite bluntly, that he *wanted* to move on—that he didn't want to stay...

And I couldn't ask that of him...

As I endured that hellish dinner, I teared up a few times, but Rick didn't notice.

Mal did.

His cheerfulness cracked—just a little. But once I found that crack, I knew for sure that this wasn't as easy for him as he was pretending.

"So I told my sister," Rick said now as he poured us both more of my shitty red wine. I glanced over at Mal who sighed—just a little—at the fact that the replenished wine glasses meant dinner was dragging on. "For the love of God, if you're gonna insist on listening to shitty pop music, at least listen to something with a horn section, you know what I mean?"

I took a sip—it may not have been expensive as far as Pinot Noir went, but it tasted good to me. "I have to confess," I told Rick, "this time I'm on your sister's side."

Rick grabbed his chest in mock horror. I knew I was supposed to laugh at his antics, so I did.

"No, really?" Rick said as he shook his head and made tsking sounds. "But okay, I understand. My sister also likes photography. You must have similarly faulty wiring in your brains."

Malcolm sat up at that. "I'm sorry... What did he just say?"

Rick was clearly only teasing.

"Very funny," I said.

Mal made a disgusted, scoffing sound. "No, it's not."

Rick grinned at me. "Yeah, I'm just kidding. I appreciate the art you've got on your walls. I do. It's just not my thing."

Malcolm looked from Rick to me to Rick. "What *is* your thing?" He looked back at me. "Ask him what his thing is."

Rick held up his glass to admire the color of the wine as he said, "I prefer my visual art to be abstract."

He took a long sip of wine as Mal shook his head.

"Or just wait a half a second for him to start talking again," Mal said. "Jesus, has this guy let you get a word in edgewise all night...? You know, he hasn't even asked you what you do for a living."

"Photos are just... too... basic," Rick told me. "Simple. I think of them as windows, you know what I mean? It's the ultimate in realism, so you might as well just cut another window into your wall, rather than hang a stupid photograph."

"He said to the professional photographer," Mal interjected.

"There's nothing wrong with having a... strong opinion." I managed to get a word or two in edgewise.

Mal remained outraged. "There is when an idiot tells the best photographer I've ever met that his brilliant art is *simple*."

Rick batted his eyes—his eyelashes were crazy long—and gave me his best fuck-me smile. "At last, someone who really sees me for me—"

"You know what I mean?" Mal said the words in unison with Rick, mimicking his delivery so pitch-perfectly that I had to laugh.

It was the first time that I'd laughed genuinely all evening. And apparently it inspired Rick to reach across the table and take my hand.

"You have a great laugh," he said, gazing at me soulfully, as I reminded myself what Mal had taught me about the perils of reaching for someone's hand. I wanted to pull away—*Don't touch me*—but Mal was right. It takes real courage to instigate a hand-hold. "And your eyes are... majestic."

Courage—or extreme self-confidence. Or maybe a combination of the two.

"*Majestic?*" Mal blew loud raspberries. "No. FYI, I've changed my mind about his hat, too. It's fucking stupid."

"He likes me," I reminded Mal—but then remembered that I shouldn't speak directly to him. Oops.

But Rick's smile only widened as he took my mistake for flirtiness.

"He does," he responded, referring to himself in the dread third person as Mal nearly eye-rolled himself to death. Assuming he could die again. "Very much, in fact. So much so that he's hoping to stay for breakfast, too."

"No." Mal's response was immediate. "Nope. Laugh in his face and tell him it's time for him to go."

I did neither. *Hundreds of years of agony...* I also still didn't pull my hand away.

Instead I took another fortifying sip of wine and told Rick, "I have a friend who recently passed who told me... well, basically he agreed with you, that life is too short to drink shitty wine."

Rick toasted me with his glass. "Your friend was right. Here's to only drinking the good wine."

"Yes," I said, and even though I was speaking to Rick and looking at Rick, my words were for Malcolm. "But I would argue, and as opinionated as you are, Rick, I think you'd agree, that a hundred years of agony is *way* worse than drinking shitty wine."

Malcolm

I flashed hot and cold as I realized what Henry had just told me.

The *shitty wine* that Henry was going to be drinking tonight, so to speak, was Rick.

It was my own damn fault for putting the idea into Henry's

head—with all my talk that his moment of connection with Rick might need to be *glorious*, i.e. orgasmic.

So yes, Henry was willing to sleep with Rick, in hopes that my unfinished business would be finished, and I'd move on—and away from those frightening centuries of pain that were at the top of most lingering spirits' to-do lists.

I stood up. "Oh, fuck, Henry, no…"

"I'm not sure I'm following," Rick said in response to Henry's twisted-sounding Yoda-tudes, "but your eyes are like two tiny universes pulling me in."

I knocked on the table, because oh, holy fucking shit… "Tiny majestic universes. This is not what I want for you—a lifetime of wearing *I'm with Stupid* T-shirts…?

Henry refused to look at me. Instead he smiled into Rick's eyes. "Even shitty wine can taste better over time. Or at least after your third glass…"

Rick nodded. "That's very profound."

Shit. As I watched, horrified, Henry leaned across the table and kissed Rick.

"No," I said. "No no no-no no-no!"

But Henry ignored me.

Smiling into Rick's eyes, he stood up—still holding Rick's hand—and tugged him up and out of his seat, and—*no!*—out of the dining room.

"I'm still here!" I pointed out. "You kissed him, but I'm still here! What are you doing? Where are you going! No. *No!*"

As I followed them, I saw that Rick had taken his wine glass with him—so much for shitty wine—he'd liked his so much he was unwilling to abandon it.

"I changed my mind," I told Henry as both jealousy and envy made my stomach churn and boil. I didn't get hungry and I couldn't eat, but it was possible I might just throw up. "I don't want you to do this!"

Henry pulled Rick into his bedroom and he shut the door firmly in my face—knowing damn well that I couldn't open it.

But then I realized…

"And *you* don't want to do this, either!" I shouted at Henry through the door. "You feel *nothing*! When you kissed me, you felt *everything*, but with *him* you feel *nothing*! I know this, because of the binding spell! I feel what you feel, remember…? And with him, *you feel nothing!*"

CHAPTER SIXTEEN
Henry

Mal was right.

I felt nothing for Rick.

Except a whole lot of shame and remorse that he was so into me, while I was merely using him as a terrible means to a terrible end. It added just that little extra-special shittiness—one of Rick's favorite words—on top of the mountain of motherfucking sadness and grief I was buried under because of Malcolm's death.

But the fact that Rick didn't notice—or maybe he'd had too much wine to care—that I was grimly, coldly detached as he attempted to take off my clothes...? That made me less remorseful.

"*I know you can hear me so open the door!*" Mal shouted from out in the hallway.

I crossed to my sound-dock and turned on some music of the "shitty pop" variety and cranked the volume—funny how Rick didn't seem to hate it now as he began dancing to the beat.

As I looked at him—so shiny and beautiful and so not Malcolm—I wondered if it would register with him at all if I suddenly broke down and cried...?

Malcolm

Henry turned on some music and turned it up loud.

"I'll be damned if I don't stop this!" I tried to shout over it. But then I realized what I'd said. "Well, I guess technically I'll be damned if I *do* stop this, but... I don't give a damn." I looked around me, a tad wildly, but in fact I was paying attention to the layout of Henry's house as well as doing math as I thought about the power behind that freaky tether from our binding spell. "Forty feet, I need forty feet..."

Henry's bedroom faced the front of the house. Its window looked out into his front yard...

Jesus, that could work! I just had to get outside.

With rising determination, I turned toward the front door, but then stopped short. It was, of course, tightly closed.

But the bolt was not thrown, so that meant...

I could do this.

I took a deep breath and I grabbed the door handle, and with a ear-splitting roar, I threw the door open.

Holy fuck, I did it!

Getting through the screen was easy, so I rushed outside and around to the bedroom window. Henry had yet to close his curtains, and oh, sweet Jesus, Rick was peering out the window, directly at me.

"*Ahhhh!*" I shouted, more startled than he was, because he couldn't see me. Henry could, of course, but his back was turned. Shit, he'd taken off his shirt...

"Whoa, it's really windy," Rick said as he looked through me. No doubt he'd heard my door-opening scream. And speaking of screaming, he was shouting, too, just to be heard over Henry's too-loud music.

"It just sounds windy," Henry shouted back. "It's... a feature of the house."

"A what...?" Rick asked. "Do you think you could maybe turn the music down a little?" He danced his way over to Henry, pulling him in for a kiss.

The sight of his hands against Henry's bare skin made me a little crazy.

"*NOOOOOO!!*" I shouted, and this time Henry heard me and looked over.

His eyes widened as he saw me. But then he crossed toward me, mouthing *Centuries of agony* and *Go away* before he sharply, abruptly closed the curtains.

But he wasn't careful, and I could still see in through a gap.

As I watched, Henry actually squared his shoulders as he headed back to Rick, who'd stripped down to his colorful underwear.

I had to admit that the man could dance. And just looking at him, through the window, he kinda was sheer perfection.

I hesitated, because maybe he'd been trying too hard during dinner. Maybe he'd had too much wine, maybe...

"I want your dick in my mouth," Rick told Henry—still shouting over the music.

Or maybe he was just an asshole.

"I bet they call you Mr. Romance," I muttered. Although, to be fair, the direct approach—*your dick, my mouth, now*—could be extremely hot, but I knew Henry well, and he wanted wooing in advance of his hot sex. He fucking deserved it, too—long, slow, deep, cherishing kisses that would make his eyes flutter closed as he sighed...

Instead, thanks to me and my hundred years of problems, he'd been given two cursory, slapdash, probably sloppy kisses before that charming offer of deep-throating.

And, yeah, when I say that aloud, it doesn't sound all *that* terrible, but you and me...? We're not Henry.

His response to Mr. Romance's offer was to shout—over the music, "That sounds... glorious."

I was well aware that he hadn't used that word by accident, and as Rick dropped to his knees in front of Henry, I'd definitely seen enough.

"*NOOOOOO!*" I shouted, knowing that while Henry heard me, Rick only heard the wind.

I ran, as hard and as fast as I could toward the street in front of Henry's house—and not just because I didn't want to see any more, although that was true, too. A few feet before the property line, I hit solid resistance with a painful, ear-ringing splat. I'd found the edge of our binding-spell's forty-foot tether and it felt like crashing into a solid but invisible wall. But unlike the Kool-Aid Man (who I'd always imagined was weird triplets with both the Stay-Puff Marshmallow Man and the Pillsbury Doughboy), I hadn't gone through it—I'd bounced back and onto the ground.

I saw stars from the impact, but I didn't let that stop me. I scrambled to my feet and—slightly more carefully this time—I re-found the place of resistance. And I pushed against it with all of my feeble spirit strength, hoping that just as Henry had dragged me behind him during his run, I might be able to move him now.

∞

Henry

What's that old saying...? *Close your eyes and think of England.*

Or rather, in this case, think of Malcolm and his need to move on.

I closed my eyes as Rick tugged my briefs down my legs. As he handled me, I gritted my teeth—his touch did the opposite of what he'd intended.

"Oh, shy, are we...?" he murmured. "Let me get your motor running..."

Oh, God, really...? I made the mistake of opening my eyes and saw Rick smiling up at me. He was so convinced that he was everything I both wanted and needed, and he could not have been more wrong.

"I'm about to blow your mind," he informed me, but before I could respond—what *was* the correct etiquette to use in this situation? *Probably not, but thank you for trying...?*—I suddenly, weirdly, fell backwards.

It was like someone had pulled me, hard, right out of Rick's grasp.

Making a graceful landing isn't ever easy when doing a back-wards long-jump, and because my underwear was around my ankles, I was even more challenged. I stumbled and fell, and then skidded backwards on my butt, my head hitting the wall beneath my front window. "Ow!"

Rick, meanwhile, went facedown onto the floor. "Ow!"

As I jerked my briefs back up and pulled myself to my feet, I also pulled the curtain back a little so I could look out the window, and sure enough, Mal was on his ass—having fallen just as I did—in the middle of my front yard.

As I watched, he scrambled to his feet, and...

He was pushing—hard—against our binding-spell tether, and he'd actually managed to yank me away from Rick. But pitting his spirit-wimpy strength against mine...? This wasn't going to work. It just wasn't.

"Malcolm, stop!" I whispered as I watched him. "What's hard for you is nothing for me."

And sure enough, it took almost no effort—now that I was focused on it—for me to counter Mal's pull. I had to dig in a little to keep my feet securely on the floor, but it wasn't much harder than walking through the drag of water in a swimming pool. I purposely went farther into the middle of my room than I had to, knowing that Mal was being pulled toward me—maybe he'd get my message—as I held out a hand to help Rick up.

"Sorry," I apologized. "I'm so clumsy."

"*NOOOOOO!*" I heard Mal shout from out in the yard.

Somehow, he did it again. I think he intentionally stopped pulling me. And because I was actively resisting him, the release made me stagger and lose my balance. But then Mal swiftly started pulling again, even harder this time, and the force of that dragged me—and made me push Rick, since he was between Mal and me—all the way across my bedroom, pinning us both against the window.

Or rather, I was pinning Rick there.

"Shit!" I shouted as Rick asked, "What the hell...?" as the curtain came down on our heads.

Rick's back and my face were both smashed against the window pane.

"What are you doing?" he exclaimed. "Get off of me!"

"I wish I could," I mumbled as I angled my head to try to get a glimpse of Mal.

He was still pushing hard against the tether, and as he glanced back at me, over his shoulder, the concentration made his face look ferocious.

"Why can't you...?" Rick asked.

"I'm stuck," I told him. I had no idea where Mal's newfound strength was coming from. Maybe it was the awkward angle in which he'd pinned me there, but I really couldn't move.

"We need a safe word," Rick told me, "if you want to role play or whatever this is..."

Out in the yard, Mal wasn't letting up.

"Malcolm!" I shouted.

"That's a weird safe word," Rick said, "but I guess it'll do. Malcolm! Malcolm!"

"No," I said. "I just... *Malcolm!*"

"*Will you stop...?*" Mal's shout from the front yard came with a hurricane-force sounding wind.

"Yes!" I shouted back.

And Mal finally let go.

I fell backwards, onto my butt again, as the tether was released.

Rick fell on top of me.

"God!" I said as Rick chimed in with "Ow! I think I pulled something."

We both scrambled away from each other. Talk about awkward...

"I'm so sorry," I said.

Rick nodded as he continued to back away. He pulled himself to his feet. "I'm... gonna go."

"That's probably best," I agreed as he yanked his pants on, grabbed his shirt, and hurried out of the room. I heard the front door open and then close with no small amount of absolute finality as my despair and rage came to a rapid boil inside of me.

And then, there he was.

Mal.

Still breathing hard. Standing in my bedroom doorway. As the music still loudly pounded.

I slapped it off, and the sudden silence was deafening.

"What is wrong with you?" I spat the words at him.

Rick was gone—and he wasn't coming back.

Mal leaned in the doorway—which pissed me off. That whole *tall drink of water* expression immediately came to mind, and I wanted to shout, *Stop looking so fucking good!*

"Friends don't let friends fuck douchebags," Mal told me.

I shot back, "Friends don't let friends suffer centuries of pain!"

Mal nodded. "Yeah, well, this was worse."

I couldn't believe what he was saying. "Than centuries of pain...?"

"Yes, all right?" He was definitely less cool and collected than he was pretending to be because he blasted me then, with: "*YEEESSS!*"

The force of Mal's shout made me stagger, and I almost hit the floor again, but he stepped into my room, reaching out to catch me.

And there we were.

Nose to nose, with his arms tightly around me. Pressed against each other from our chests to our knees. He was taller than me by a little bit, and he was broader, too. He was so solidly, deliciously Mal that my body responded instantly.

There was no way he didn't feel it—I was standing there in only my briefs. But even though I was steady now, he didn't let me go— he just looked into my eyes, as if searching for some kind of easy answer to this bullshit we were dealing with.

"Mal, I was trying to help you," I whispered. "You said this was what you wanted."

"Yeah, well, I was lying," he admitted. "And *you* were lying, too. When you kissed him, I could feel it—that you don't even like the guy, that you can't possibly love him... I knew—because it didn't feel like *this* when you kissed him."

Mal's gaze dropped only briefly to my mouth—that was the only warning I got before he pulled me even closer and kissed me.

And he was right, because my heart raced and my brain stuttered and every single cell in my body celebrated. My very soul went into dizzying, crazy-wonderful free-fall because I didn't just want him, I *needed* him, and he was finally kissing me...

"God, you love me," Mal pulled back—just a little—to whisper, his breath warm and sweet across my lips. He kissed me again—more gently now, but no less thoroughly, and this time when he pulled back, it was so that he could look into my eyes. His own were haunted—and filled with tears. "I feel it, and... I didn't know how badly I wanted that before, because..." He could barely get the words out. "I love you, too."

He tried to release me, to turn away, but I caught his face between my hands. "I do love you," I told him. "Present tense."

I kissed him then, and he kissed me back so hungrily that I couldn't help but laugh a little, despite the sorrow and heartache I knew we both were feeling.

"I just wish we'd had this conversation before dinner," I told him, trying to make him laugh as I deepened my voice to sound like Rick. "You know what I mean?"

Mal did laugh at that, but I knew that he was still terribly torn.

So I kissed him again.

"I want you to have someone," he told me between kisses. "I don't want you to be alone, and I thought... The *Book* says that all spirits disconnect. We stop worrying about the people we've left behind. So I just keep waiting to stop worrying—to stop caring about you. But every fucking minute that passes, it just hurts more." He stepped back and this time kept me at arm's length to tell me, "God, I finally have a real reason to stay the hell away from you— you need to be with someone who's not dead—and it's breaking my heart."

I shook my head and poured twelve years of desire and longing into each kiss, each touch—my fingers in his hair, on his back, on his ass as I pulled him more tightly against me.

And I felt his resistance dissolve—and in our current reality, that was not normally a happy word. But right now it was incredible as he stopped fighting and surrendered to this moment that we were sharing—this gift of borrowed time that we'd somehow miraculously been given.

The sensation of his hands sliding down my shoulders and back—against my bare skin—took my breath away.

Together we sank down onto my bed.

Malcolm

I can't eat cake, remember, so I wasn't quite sure exactly how this was going to work.

But since soul-kissing Henry was already on my short Can-Do-Despite-Being-Dead list, my hopes were high.

Embracing the moment definitely helped. I mean, sure, I could've spent the entire time sobbing because I'd stupidly waited to do this until after I was dead. I was never going to forgive myself for that, but I had an eternity to beat myself up.

Right now...?

Henry was mine, and I lost myself in kissing and touching him.

But I know you're probably curious about the logistics of our hot man-on-ghost action.

Could I even take off my clothes—my so-called *ghost outfit* that I was wearing when I'd died...? To be honest, I hadn't tried before this. I no longer needed to pee, so I hadn't so much as unzipped my jeans. And before you start screaming about hygiene, it simply wasn't an issue.

Yeah, I'd been dragged around the neighborhood while on that run with Henry, and I'd been literally a hot mess afterwards. Some of that heavy lifting that I'd done—the button pushing and toilet-paper pulling—had also made me break into a serious sweat. But I blinked, and it was gone. And my clothes were just instantly as fresh as they'd been when I'd apparently died.

So file *that* under "Weird New Rules," along with the whole Henry-stubs-his-toe-and-I-say-*Ow*-too thing.

And I'm not sure if it was the binding spell that made it so, but as Henry and I tumbled back onto his bed, my clothes came off quite easily and quickly. Henry even helped, which was lovely. Full confession: I had a small amount of trouble with his briefs—while Henry was wearing them, I had no problem. I easily dragged them down his long legs—taking my time only because I wanted to. It was *after* I'd pulled them off him that my relationship with them changed to spirit-slash-exceedingly-heavy-inanimate-object. They went from being as light as a pair of briefs to seeming to weigh about two hundred pounds.

The momentum pulled me backwards and off the bed. I landed on the floor with Henry's briefs on my chest, pinning me down, and he'd had to come and save me.

It was funny—we both laughed at the slapstick absurdity. But a little red flag popped up in the back of my mind. If that had happened pre-binding spell, while I was still invisible to Henry, I would've been stuck there until he'd decided to do his laundry.

And God forbid I got pinned under something that wouldn't get moved for five or ten years. And feel free to judge away, but *some* of us keep our homes clean enough by vacuuming around piles of files or books or even that weird cat statue our Great-Aunt Thomasina gave us when we were seven, but we kept it because it looks remarkably like Princess Leia at certain angles.

Anyway, as I'm sure you can imagine, my red flag wasn't the only thing that popped up as Henry and I both successfully got naked.

It seemed surreal. We'd been friends for so long. But apparently I'd compartmentalized both my attraction and desire for years, because now that that door was wide open, it all came exploding out.

I was consumed by my need for this man.

I know that, right about now, you're remembering I not only didn't get hungry, but I physically couldn't eat. (See *Attempt to eat candy-corn-cake icing, Malcolm, Chapter Five, above.*)

Yet, as we kissed, I tasted Henry, and it was lovely. Now, it's possible that I couldn't really taste his kisses, but that the binding spell plus our intimacy allowed me to taste what he was tasting. (If that's the case, I tasted lovely to him, which was nice to know.)

At least that was my theory. He'd eaten a steak while sitting right in front of me a few hours ago, and I hadn't tasted anything. Of course, at the time I was dealing with the bad-taste-in-my-mouth that was Rick and his hatred of photography.

But… maybe if Henry ate a piece of cake whilst shagging me, I'd be able to get at least a glimmer of the sweetness. Note to self: *Try that later.* Right now, however, Henry himself was all the sweetness I needed.

After the underwear-knocked-me-onto-the-floor fiasco, we both spent quite a bit of time just kissing and touching. I discovered I had a long-held secret desire to lick Henry all over, but as I started with his throat and collarbone, I realized that my tongue didn't leave a trail of wetness behind. I licked him, but he was instantly dry.

But my mouth didn't feel dry.

I experimented by spitting on his chest—and yeah, Henry responded as you might imagine anyone would when a first-time lover suddenly spits on their chest.

He propped himself up on his elbows and half-laughed as he gave me his classic *What the fuck* face.

"Yeah, that was weird, sorry," I said as I ran my hand across his exceedingly well-defined pecs and showed it to him: dry. "But it suddenly occurred to me that… well, I'm not sure I can ejaculate."

It was a valid concern, since I no longer needed to void or eliminate. (That's fancy-talk for pee and poop.)

And I know what you're thinking. What the living hell, Malcolm, isn't this supposed to be the big romantic love scene…? Shouldn't you be using words like *throbbing* and *orgasmic* instead of *ejaculation, void,* and *eliminate*? The earth should be moving and choirs of angels should be singing. Can't you at least wax poetic about two hearts connecting, two souls becoming one?

You should be telling Henry, *You complete me,* or *I like you, very much. Just as you are.*

Not, *I'm not sure I can ejaculate…*

Way to be super-sexy and romantic, ass-hat.

But Henry didn't laugh at me. In fact, his eyes quite possibly turned a warmer shade of blue. "I bet you can," he said. "Or at least you'll be able to feel it—with a spirit-world bonus: No wet-spot…?"

I kissed him. I could always count on Henry to find the bright side.

But then he reached down and wrapped his hand around me. "Do you feel this?" he asked as he stroked me.

And yeah, oh my God. I nodded because I suddenly couldn't

speak, it felt so good. Henry's eyes flared with both heat and satisfaction as he leaned in and soul-kissed me.

And I felt...

I felt...

Whoa, wait a motherfucking minute...

I pulled away from both his mouth and his hand, and manhandled him onto his back, because I need to see if...

His dick was a thing of beauty—hard and large and I would've loved to take my time and introduce myself more properly, but right now I was in a bit of a hurry, so I took just the tip of him into my mouth and gave an experimental swirl with my tongue and...

The sensation was so intense, I nearly went through the roof.

I did it again, and again we both moaned.

"Oh, God," I told Henry breathlessly. "The binding spell... I feel everything you feel."

Henry laughed as realization widened his eyes. If I could feel it when Henry stubbed his toe, then I could also feel it when *dot dot dot*...

"*Every*thing...?" His voice cracked.

"God, yes!" I laughed, too, as I went down on us both. "Holy fuck, I've found the sole perk of being dead!"

Jesus, this was crazy and intense—feeling everything that Henry felt.

I mean, I've always really enjoyed sex. What's not to love? It feels great, and then it feels *really* great, and you laugh and smile a lot while you're doing it. Even the shittiest sex feels good, so generally it's an activity in which everyone wins.

But sex with Henry was...

There's really no right word to describe it, because... all of his intense pleasure...? *I* was making him feel that way. And sure, when you're having sex, you kind of know that doing what you're doing will make your lover feel good. But you're really just going on faith. You don't *really* know. Maybe they secretly hate it and they're just faking enjoyment.

But with Henry, because of the binding spell, I knew precisely how good I was making him feel.

I also knew that Henry truly loved me. God, *that* was...

It's another thing that you just take on faith—when someone says they love you. You have no idea how they define love—what it means to them, or just how casually they might toss the word out there with little thought as to its impact. Someone else's *I love you* might mean *Yeah, I love you a solid, oh,* five, *right below that six-star pizza we had when we went to Boston.*

But Henry *loved* me. He loved me a million—with every cell in his body, with every beat of his heart.

A lot like the way I loved him.

So take that, then add in the physical effects of the binding spell...?

I lifted my head and managed to form words and say them aloud. "I gotta get inside you," I told Henry.

He immediately knew why he should be the one to bottom, and was already going for the lube he kept in his bedside table drawer.

And... the lube was a slight issue. When Henry put it on me—because I couldn't do it myself—my dick suddenly weighed a million pounds. We wiped that shit off fast. But, like his briefs, once it was on Henry it didn't affect me. I mean, it affected me, enormously, in that it lubricated and allowed me to...

So, maybe this is where I should start flinging around phrases like *Our souls became one.*

Because our fucking souls abso-fucking-lutely became fucking one as I pushed myself inside of Henry and found his prostate with an accuracy that would've been impossible without the binding spell.

So not only was I instantly the best lover Henry had ever known—partly because I was feeling everything that he was—but I was also feeling what *I* was feeling. Which would've been incredible all by itself. Instead, it was kinda like having a three-way with Henry and myself.

Including the double-orgasm.

Yeah.

Henry came first, and as his release crashed through me, it pushed me over the edge.

I started to laugh—I couldn't help it. And that got Henry laughing, too.

And if wanting and wishing alone could bring me back to life, it would've happened—right then and there.

CHAPTER SEVENTEEN
Malcolm

The immediate aftermath of first-sex is tricky enough to navigate when both partners are alive.

After the euphoria starts to fade, reality rears its ugly head and doubt comes creeping in.

I stared at the ceiling above Henry's bed, mired in dark thoughts.

"That was… glorious."

I turned to find Henry watching me—his eyes so serious despite the small smile that played about his lips.

"It was," I agreed. "Although I guess that means shagging you wasn't my *powerful unfinished business*."

Henry put his hand on my chest—warm and grounding—as he nodded. "I'm glad. I'm not ready for you to go anywhere."

As he leaned in to kiss me, my heart clenched. I pushed myself up on one elbow, because, yeah, we had to have this conversation, and it might as well be right now.

I chose my words carefully. "I'm not sure you've thought that through."

Jesus, I'd done this so many times with so many different men. *Well*, that *was fun, but dot dot dot*. Also known as the *Here's why this will never work* speech. Usually delivered with a sense of relief and shame not unlike the feeling that comes after eating an entire sleeve of Chips Ahoy. Shame, because, Jesus, that was both selfish and self-indulgent. Relief because I'd stopped after only one—I didn't go for the two-sleeve, full-box, self-loathing experience.

But this time, I felt only an almost unbearable sadness. Especially because I knew that Henry had started this discussion to convince me—well, I wasn't sure of exactly *what*, but I was about to find out. But nothing he could say would counter the fact that I was dead.

Of course, he started his argument by addressing that head-on. "What's the big deal?" Henry shrugged. "You're a ghost, but so what."

"*So what...?*" I laughed. "How about, I can't be more than forty feet away from you at all times. And there's that whole feeling-like-I'm-gonna-dissolve-if-we-get-too-far-from-the-house thing. How, exactly, are you going to go to work?"

That logistic was one Henry obviously hadn't considered, but he rose to the challenge.

"I'll... turn the garage into a studio," he said, leaping outside of the box in true Henry fashion. "Clients will come to me."

I laughed in his adorable face. "To get married? In your garage. Kinda puts a new spin on *Destination Wedding.*"

He knew he was on the losing side of that argument, so he abandoned it and tried: "I'll... specialize in engagement photos."

"Again, in your garage?" I shot him down. "Your clients want to work with you because of your incredible outdoor shots. On the beach, in the desert, in the mountains..." All places I couldn't go, and that meant he couldn't go there, either.

Henry refused to surrender. "So... I'll take some time off. I have money saved."

Nice try, but I came back with, "Enough for forever? Cause I'll be here forever. And hello, you eat. How are you gonna get groceries?"

"I'll get food delivered."

Okay, that part of the problem had a solution, but it was just one tiny part. "Henry," I said.

He reached up and put his hand against my face, making sure I couldn't look away from him as he responded in the exact same tone, "Mal." But then he added, "Please. Can we maybe just bask in the glow of the glory for a few more minutes...?"

I was the one who surrendered then. I could, at least, give him that. I put my arms around him and pulled him against me, and we spooned as Henry sighed and closed his eyes.

"I've wanted this for so long," he murmured.

He sighed again—and then almost instantly fell asleep.

How the hell did he do that?

It was both maddening and endearing, and for a moment, I couldn't breathe, because I wanted to be not-dead so goddamn badly. I wanted to wake Henry up and say *Teach me how to live in this crazy world so effortlessly and joyfully.* I wanted to tell him, *Please love me just like this, forever, and don't ever leave me...*

But I'd already left *him.*

"This isn't real," I whispered to the beautiful man sleeping in my arms. "And it's not fair to you."

Still, I lay there for a while, just holding Henry, his *So what* ringing in my head as I tried to think the way he always did—how could we make this work…? I kept coming back to the binding spell, and I finally—gently so as not to wake him—got out of bed.

My clothes were where I'd left them on the floor—taking them off had been a little scary. Would they vanish? Was I about to become a naked ghost? Imagine dying in the shower or while having sex—and being naked forever. Jesus. That would suck.

As I pulled on my T-shirt, I went into the living room where Henry's laptop was out and open. I sat in front of it and took several deep, cleansing breaths before I used all of my strength to type into the *Crimson Book's* search engine, one exhausting letter at a time: "How… to… break… a… binding… spell."

One more herculean push to hit enter and…

I caught my breath as I leaned in closer to look at the screen.

Henry

When I woke up in the night, Malcolm was gone.

I sat up with a gasp in my empty bed, fearing the worst as I called out, "Mal…?"

"I'm out here, babe." His familiar voice floated back to me from the living room.

Oh, thank God. I sagged with relief.

I got out of bed and found my clothes and yanked them on as I went to find him—to make sure he hadn't gone into panic mode. It was his pattern—he'd told me so, many times. He'd connect with a man, have really great sex, and then he'd run screaming into the night.

He was sitting in front of my laptop as I went into the living room, but he stood up and closed it, almost furtively, as I approached.

"*Now* you wear clothes," he quipped, but his smile seemed forced.

"What are you doing?" I asked.

"Well, since I don't sleep…"

"Right," I said. "Sorry."

But then he told me, "I remembered that you left the house. Back before we did the binding spell. You drove."

Holy crap, he was right. Right after he'd gone missing, I'd used my car to drive… "To hospitals and…" I had to clear my throat. "Morgues. Yeah." I'd left the house, and Mal hadn't been dragged along behind me, the way he'd been when I'd gone for a run after invoking the binding spell.

The binding spell made it possible for me to see, hear, and touch Mal, but it also apparently created our weird tether. It was possible that the sensation he'd described as being about to evaporate or dissolve the farther he got from my house was another side effect of that spell.

But even if it wasn't…

Mal had been thinking exactly the same thing. "I was checking the *Crimson Book*," he told me, "to see if we could break the binding spell. Just temporarily. Turn it off so you could go to work, then back on when you come home…?"

"That's brilliant!" I said.

But Mal didn't share my excitement. "In theory, yes. In reality, no. The book says it's one and done. We un-do this, it's forever. The spell is… used up."

That was disappointing news. It was also extremely worrying. "Then we better never un-do it."

Malcolm sighed. "Henry, I'm dead."

"I don't care," I told him. "We'll make it work. We'll figure it out."

He was looking at me—like, really looking, as if he was trying to memorize my face.

But then he sighed almost theatrically and shrugged, and with his hands out, he said, "Except, you know what? I was wrong."

I was about to make a joke—*What, you, wrong? Impossible!*

But I didn't do more than open my mouth to speak when he added, "About *you* not being my unfinished business. Because the, uh, portal to the spirit world has opened."

I laughed. Oh, I'd heard the words he'd said, but after I ran them through the Mal-speak translator, his tone plus the way he was standing made me hear: *I'm making a big, giant joke.*

Except, Mal didn't laugh with me. In fact, for a moment he

looked annoyed. Then he clutched his pearls—he literally put his hands at the base of his throat—and gasped as he gazed up at the ceiling. That only made me laugh more—he was obviously trying to be funny, right...?

"Yes!" he intoned. "The portal is opening and..."

I turned to look where Mal was looking and saw only my living room ceiling. The room was an add-on built in the late 1960s, and the ceiling had a very slight vault with exposed, rustic beams that screamed *feelin' groovy*.

"The light is so beautiful," Mal said, still staring up there, as if transfixed.

"Wait." I stopped laughing. "Are you serious?"

He drifted past me, arms reaching up. "I'm being pulled toward the light. But, I'm, um, resisting it..."

I went from laughing to fully freaked out, and when I grabbed his arm to help him, he clung to me.

"I don't want to leave you." Mal's voice broke.

"Then don't go," I said. "Tell whatever's up there to close the door. Your business is *not* finished here."

Mal grabbed my face between his hands and kissed me.

"But it is," he said quietly. "You know, now, that I love you. And we had last night—which was everything to me. And I *do* have to go, because I'm dead and you're not."

He kissed me again, so damn sweetly, and my mind spun and stuttered. And despite my knee-jerk reaction of *Please don't leave me*, I heard what he was telling me. He *had* to go...

"Just promise me that you won't give up," Mal told me. "That you'll find someone who loves you..."

"Mal," I said.

"...as much as I did." He kissed me again.

"Please, no," I begged him. "I want more time."

He nodded, but then shook his head. "I know this is hard—it's really hard for me, too, but I need your help to get through the portal. I need you to say these words. In Latin. You have to say it— it won't work for me. And, well... I love you. Be happy."

God, I didn't want him to suffer. If he stayed, I'd have him for the next few decades—seven at the most. I mean, realistically. After that, *I'd* be dead, and unless we could use the *Crimson Book* to figure out how to turn me into a ghost, and keep *me* from moving on, too...

But one thing Pat's *Crimson Book* had made very clear was that spirits who lingered were rare. Most people died and immediately, instantly moved on. And if I did *that*—and odds were that I *would* when my time came—I'd abandon Mal to those goddamned centuries of pain.

So, nope. I couldn't risk that.

As much as I wanted more time with Mal, he wanted to go right now and he needed my help to do it.

So I did what he asked me. My eyes filled with tears and I braced for him to vanish as I translated *I love you. Be happy* into Latin. *"Te amo. Es laetus."*

Malcolm laughed—a bark of surprise. "No, H, that was *me* saying that to *you*, that wasn't the Latin I need you to..." He stopped. "Wait, you know Latin...?"

"Yeah," I told him. "I took it in high school."

He'd been gazing soulfully at me, but now he closed his eyes. "Fuuuhhhck." He let go of me, too.

I couldn't help but notice that even though I wasn't holding him down, he didn't immediately drift upwards toward the portal. In fact, now he wasn't paying any attention at all to the *beautiful light* from just beyond my Jimi-Hendrix-era ceiling.

"What exactly *is* the Latin you want me to say?" I asked him suspiciously.

Mal cleared his throat. "Just, you know..." He lowered his voice to a barely audible mutter. *"Vinculum abrumperes. Terminus est fabula. Terminus est nunc...?"*

My mouth dropped open. Even with my incredibly rusty Latin, I knew... "Fucking sever the fucking bond...?" I asked him.

He forced a smile. "I'm pretty sure the fucking part's not in there."

"Fucking end the fucking story...?" My head exploded. "That sounds an awful lot like something you'd say to break, oh, I don't know, a *binding spell*...?"

Malcolm

Henry was rip-shit.

And rightfully so.

"Yes," I admitted. "That's... Yes."

"There's not really a portal," he asked, "with beautiful light, is there?"

I scratched my head. "No. I... made that up."

Henry just stood there, looking at me with his giant blue anime-character eyes, like I'd just killed his puppy. Or worse.

"Wow," he whispered. "You must really not want to be with me. Oh, my God."

What...? "No!" I told him. "That's not why I..." Jesus, did he *really* think...? "Henry, I love you! I do! I want to stay—I want to stay so badly! I just... You deserve to be with someone who's alive."

And there it was. My heart—torn from my chest and thrown, exposed, onto the floor in front of him.

Or maybe—from the look on Henry's face—that was *his* heart down there, and I'd managed to not only tear it from *his* chest, but I'd just stomped all over it, too. Look at me—screwing things up, right on schedule.

And when Henry finally spoke, his voice was shredded with both his anger and his pain.

"Fuck you, Malcolm," he said. "Why do *you* get to decide what I deserve...? You couldn't take ten minutes to have a conversation with me about this? You just made up your mind to... to... trick me into breaking the binding spell? And then what? You'd be here, but I wouldn't know it. Someday—probably very soon, because living here without you would suck—I'd move out, thinking you gone to Pat's place of fucking peace. But you'd still be here, at the start of centuries of agony while I thought you were somewhere safe." He shook his head and whispered, "How could you do that to me?"

Dear God... "I didn't think about... that..."

Henry exploded. "Because you didn't talk to me!"

I needed him to understand. "All I could think was, I can't let you ruin your life by being tied to a dead man forever! And I knew if I waited, I'd *never* leave. But God, I want better for you! I've always wanted something better for you then, you know... me."

Henry made the kind of noise you'd make if someone punched you, hard, in the stomach. But then he just stood there, looking at me.

And when he finally spoke, he said, "And there it is. The reason we've only had one night together, instead of twelve *years* of nights.

And you know what, Mal? You're right. I *do* deserve better. I deserve someone who loves me enough to fucking fight for me."

He turned away from me, ready to flee the room, unwilling to let me see him break down and cry.

But I caught his arm and didn't let him go, instead pulling him into a desperate embrace.

"I'm so sorry," I whispered. With my face pressed tightly against the warmth of his neck, I begged him, "Please forgive me. I thought I *was* fighting for you."

I felt him nod, felt him take several ragged breaths. But then he pulled back—just enough to look into my eyes.

"You want to *really* fight for me?" he asked. "Then fight for yourself. Fight for *us*. Let's not give up until we've read every fucking page of Pat's seven-hundred dollar e-book."

I had to laugh at that, but it came out sounding more like a hiccup or a sob. "Babe, it has infinity pages."

Henry nodded fiercely. "Exactly."

As I looked into his eyes, I realized what he was telling me—that he would never give up. That he would never lose hope. That he loved me *that* much.

I kissed him.

And then I pulled him back to bed, where I showed him just how much I loved him, too.

CHAPTER EIGHTEEN
Malcolm

Henry's phone was ringing again.

It was morning, and had been for awhile, but he was still sleeping. I was sitting up beside him on the bed, his head against my side, his arm draped across me. After we'd made love, he'd wanted me to stay close, and after screwing things up so badly, I was glad to give him that.

But he'd brought his laptop in so that while he slept I'd make progress on *Project: Read Every Fucking Page of Pat's Seven-Hundred Dollar e-Book*.

So far I'd discovered two things. A) Because I could touch and move Henry's hand without effort, I could use Henry's finger to turn the book's pages without having to heave and sweat. And B) Henry slept so soundly that I could use his finger to turn pages without waking him up.

As far as finding the solution to our *I'm dead, you're not* romantic conflict, I'd discovered absolutely nothing that we didn't already know.

Henry stirred just as the phone stopped ringing.

"Pretty sure it's Gina," I told him as he lifted his head.

It started ringing again.

"Who else would call this early in the morning, three times in a row," I said.

Henry found his phone. "It's not that early." He answered it, sinking back into his pillow and closing his eyes. "Yeah. I'm here. Hi. Gina."

Ding. That name-use was for me—letting me know I'd gotten it right.

"No," Henry said wearily, "I don't know how much it costs to call from Japan and…" He paused, no doubt to let her yell at him. "You're right. I failed you. I didn't check my email. Forget about the fact that I've had a lot going on." He paused again, then said,

"Well, for one thing, Mal and I had a huge fight, and then we had to make up, which was lovely—"

Something Gina told him made him suddenly open his eyes and sit up.

"What?" Henry said. He laughed. "He can't be... No, Gina, whoever killed him has his phone. That's what's going on. They're probably posting old photos so it looks like he's still alive and..." He sighed. "Okay, okay..."

With an apologetic look at me, Henry reached for his laptop and bookmarked my page as he told me, "Gina wants me to look at your freaking Facebook."

What...? Why...? "I haven't posted there in years," I told him. After finding out the social media site's insidious privacy violations, I'd stayed away. I'd yet, however, to delete my account.

Henry still used his own page regularly—as a wedding photographer it was a necessity. And we were, of course, "friends."

"She says you posted last night—that you're in Las Vegas," he informed me as he called up the log-in page. He then spoke into the phone, "He can't be in Vegas, he's with me."

That comment got some noise from Gina, but he raised his voice to speak over her. "*Yes*, right now. I'm putting you on speaker."

Henry put down his phone so he could use both hands to type in his email and password.

His Facebook page appeared as Gina's voice came through the phone, loud and clear. "Hurry. I'm bleeding money here."

"I'm hurrying," Henry told her, typing my name into the search bar.

"I can't remember the last time I went to Vegas," I said. "Maybe... two or three years ago...?"

My profile appeared on the computer screen, and Henry and I both leaned in closer to look at it, because...

"What the fuck...?" I asked.

"Who the hell is that...?" Henry asked as he flipped through a series of photos—all posted last night.

I shook my head. I had no idea. It was definitely me in those pictures—or at least it was a very good fake-me. I was definitely in Vegas, but my arm was around the shoulders of a man I swear I've never met. He was pretty damn cute—with dark hair and lively brown eyes. I *definitely* would've remembered him, but... Nope.

"It's clearly his new boyfriend," Gina responded. By *his* she meant me—*my* new boyfriend.

"No, it's not." I said the obvious.

"You really don't recognize him?" Gina asked Henry, because of course she couldn't hear me.

Henry shook his head. "No. And Mal doesn't either."

Gina exploded. "Henry, oh my God! What kind of proof do you need...?"

I leaned in to look more closely as Henry flipped through the photos again. "Jesus, what am I wearing...?"

One of the pictures—of me standing with the cute guy in front of the famous dancing fountains—had lighting that featured my clothing rather prominently. And yes, my jacket was made from some kind of shiny material that I wouldn't be caught dead in.

Okay, add *that* to my list of things I needed to stop saying.

Still... add those pants and... what the hell were those shoes...?

In another shot, we were at a roulette table—I've never played roulette in my life. And yet, there was I was behind a stack of chips, the dark-haired man at my side.

In a third, the man and I were in what looked like the lobby of a very expensive hotel, mugging while I held up a pair of... it looked like tickets...? To some kind of show...?

Henry, meanwhile, was arguing with Gina. "Just because this was posted last night doesn't mean—"

"That you're not in deep denial?" she said, sharply cutting him off. "Yes, actually, it does. Look more closely at the one where Mal's holding those VIP tickets."

Henry sighed. "I really don't want to..."

"Do it!" Gina shouted at him. "Now! Look at the date!"

With another sigh of long-suffering, Henry clicked on the photo from the hotel lobby, and enlarged it, zooming in on the tickets. I was holding them so that the printing on them was mostly legible.

"November third," Henry read.

In the photo, my thumb obscured the year.

"Two nights ago," Gina announced.

"Or," Henry said, "a *year* and two nights ago."

"Nope," Gina was absolute. "That show just opened last week. Those tickets cost around three thousand dollars each, by the way."

I screamed. "Are you fucking kidding me...?" *Three* thousand... *Each*...?

"Mal's not a ghost because he's not dead," Gina told Henry.

"He's in Vegas, the little shit, maxing out his credit cards. It's time to step back into reality, stop hallucinating, and move on already."

I was hyperventilating. Three thousand dollars times two…

Henry was looking from me to the pictures to me to the pictures with no small amount of agitation. "Gina," he said, his voice shaking, "I have to go."

He reached for his phone as Gina shouted, "Henry, wait! No, no, wait—" But he ended the call and turned to me with a look on his face that I will never forget.

His eyes were lit up and he practically shook with excitement as he told me. "She's right. You're not dead."

Those weren't the words I'd expected him to say, and they broke through the endless loop of *three thousand dollars each what the fuck, three thousand dollars each what the fuck* that was playing in my head.

I blinked at him. "I'm not…?"

He nodded vigorously. "I don't know how your body got to Vegas, but if your body's in Vegas, racking up charges on your credit card…? You're definitely not dead."

I wasn't following his logic, and he knew it. "Your credit card," he said. "What's the bank? Let's check your current charges."

I still didn't see how that would help. "My wallet's been stolen."

Still, I gave him the info he wanted, plus my password. And there it all was on my account. Holy fuck—not just the charge for those VIP tickets, but hundreds of dollars spent at a high end clothing store, crazy-expensive dinners and hotel rooms… "Notify them that someone's using my card," I told Henry.

"No," he said, "I don't want to do that yet."

"Whoever killed me is using it to—"

"Either whoever killed you looks *exactly* like you—and what are the odds of that," he pointed out, then said it again. "Or you're not dead."

Henry

Hope began to bloom in Malcolm's eyes as I signed out of his credit card account and went back to the *Crimson Book*. He couldn't sit still and started to pace.

Although my hands hovered over my keyboard. I wasn't really sure where to start.

But then my phone rang again. It wasn't Gina, calling back as I'd expected. It was...

"Hey, Pat!" I said after I punched open the connection. "Just the person I need to talk to! You're on speaker with Malcolm and me."

"I'm really not dead...?" Mal mused.

"Gina just texted and asked me to call you," Pat said. "I've only got a few minutes, but she's *very* concerned—"

I stopped her right there. "I think we were wrong and Mal's not really dead. Because his body's in Las Vegas while his spirit's still here with me. Is that even possible...?"

There was surprised silence from the other end of the phone. I just waited.

"Well," Pat finally said, "it *might* be the result of a demonic possession..."

"Demonic possession." I typed it into the *Book's* search, and tens of thousands of entries came up. "Oh my God, Mal, did you hear that?"

Mal was starting to get excited. "Yes. I'm not dead, I'm possessed by a demon. Wait, that doesn't sound good..."

"But it's very rare," Pat continued, "and it really only happens when the vessel imprisoning a demon is somehow unlocked."

"Whoa, wait, slow down!" I said. She was using a lot of terminology that was new to me. "How do you unlock a vessel? And what's a *vessel*, you mean like a boat?"

"No, no, no!" Pat said. "A vessel is... Well, I'm sure you're familiar with the legend of the genie in the lantern."

"Yes, we've seen *Aladdin*, Pat," Mal said impatiently. "Just tell us what the fuck a vessel is!"

But Pat was in full professor-mode, and I wanted to hear this so I gestured for Mal to be quiet. "The genie is a type of demon," she lectured, "and the lantern is the vessel in which he's trapped."

I got it. "Okay."

"In that specific case," Pat continued her lesson, "the vessel was unlocked, at least temporarily, when the lantern was polished or rubbed."

And *that* made sense, too.

"There are *many* types of vessels," she informed us, "with different, individual ways to unlock them. Anything from, say, shaking the vessel to reciting a simple spell. *Open sesame.*"

"Shaking the vessel...?" Mal repeated, turning to look at me with his eyes wide. "Holy fuck, on Halloween...

"Malcolm shook the orb!" I remembered.

"Well, there it is," Pat said. "A crystal orb is the most common vessel used to contain demons." Her voice then got softer, as if she'd covered her phone's mic to speak to someone else. "Oh, is it time...?" Her voice was louder again. "I'm sorry, it's time. I have to go, the ceremony is about to start. Goodbye, Henry, Malcolm. Peace to you both!"

"Pat!" I said. "Wait! How do we get the demon back into the orb...?" I looked at my phone. "Shit! She hung up."

"Check the *Crimson Book!*" Mal said.

I was already on it. But with the info we'd just gotten from Pat, I could now narrow it down...

"Demonic possession, comma, orb," I recited as I typed the words. "Let's learn how this motherfucker works."

As Mal paced, I read from the screen. "Okay, first thing that comes up: *Never shake the orb.*"

"Too late," Mal said.

"*When the orb is red,*" I read.

"The orb is red!"

"*The demon has escaped, and the hostage body's spirit must linger nearby.*"

I looked up at Mal, and he stopped pacing to turn and look at me.

"Hostage body's spirit!" We both said it at the same time.

Mal was not a dead person's *lingering spirit.* He was a demon's *hostage-body spirit.*

"I'm really not dead!" Mal said, again exactly as I said, "You're really not dead!"

We both started to laugh, and I pushed aside the laptop. I leapt off the bed and damn near tackled him, and we both jumped around the room with incredible joy.

Mal kissed me—and I kissed him back. The idea of having *You're not really dead* sex was pretty damn appealing, but there was still a shit-ton of research to do.

So I pulled away from him, and went back to the computer, again reading aloud while I typed, "How to rescue the hostage body, comma, demonic possession, comma, orb!"

Mal kept dancing as I scrolled through pages of information, reading aloud the bits that seemed relevant. "We have to break the orb."

"Great," Mal said. "Let's go break it!"

"Wait." It wasn't that simple. Holy crap, I didn't like what I was seeing, and I looked up to make sure Mal wasn't reading over my shoulder. But he'd danced his way over to the other side of the room. "First... we'll need to lure the demon and its hostage body back here."

That stopped Mal's happy dance. "How the hell do we do that?"

I gave him a reassuring smile. This was the part I knew I could handle. "I know exactly how to lure someone who buys three-thousand dollar VIP tickets." I looked closer at the *Book's* instructions. "But, Jesus, we're gonna need a shit-ton of salt."

CHAPTER NINETEEN
Malcolm

Henry's neighbor, Paul—the hot-dad of sick-on-Halloween-Joey, as opposed to the hot douche—came through in a major way.

One quick phone call—Joey was feeling much better and was back in school—and thirty minutes later, Paul was pulling into Henry's driveway.

I followed Henry outside and watched as Paul took a heavy box—filled with cartons of table salt—from the backseat of his dad-mobile.

"Thanks, Paul," Henry said as Paul put the box into his arms. "I don't have any cash on me right now, but—"

"Don't even think about it," Paul cut him off. "This was far less expensive than the mountain of candy you gave me on Halloween. Also, your timing was perfect. I was just about to head out to the store." His smile broadened. "As long as you're not cooking meth."

Henry laughed at the joke, but he didn't tell the man why he needed all that salt. I suppose it would've been awkward. *Nope, just need to create a whole bunch of salt circles in an attempt to get my boyfriend's body back from the demon who stole it after escaping his orb...*

Unfortunately, Henry's lack of explanation made Paul nervous enough to stop smiling and ask, "You're *not* cooking meth, are you?"

Was salt really an ingredient of meth? File *that* under things I didn't want to know.

"No." Henry laughed again, and this time he volunteered a decent-sounding reason for needing that shit-ton of salt. "I'm using it to get rid of... a pest."

"Oh," Paul said, the way one says *Oh* when a neighbor brings up the presence of pests.

Here in SoCal *pests* could be anything from spiders to rats to rattlesnakes to vegan anti-vaxxers.

And can I just say: Good job not-lying, Henry! That was actually very accurate without being too embarrassingly truthful.

He'd also said the word *pest* with just the right inflection to keep Paul from both asking more questions and lingering.

"Good luck with that!" Paul called, already back in his car, which was presumably completely pest-free. No doubt he wanted to keep it that way.

We waved as he drove away, then took the salt inside and got to work.

The key was in hiding the salt circle so that the demon wouldn't see it.

Because, you know, what demon is gonna say "Oh, look, a salt circle!" and then step blithely into it, right...?

Since the salt cartons were too heavy for poor little hostage-body-spirit-me, I watched and tried not to back-seat salt-circle, as Henry did the not-so-heavy lifting.

The first circle he made was just inside the front door. And it was more of an oval than a circle, but a quick consult with the *Crimson Book* confirmed that an oval was *Just fine.*

Henry covered it completely with his door mat.

Next up was his kitchen. His circle there was more salt-amoeba, but again the *CB* said *Thumbs up.*

He covered that one with a tarp—as if he were having work done in his kitchen. He added a paint can from his garage as a prop.

We went from there into Henry's living room.

As I watched, Henry rolled up his area rug and made the biggest salt-circle of them all, right there on his living room floor. He then unrolled his rug to conceal it.

With that, he exhaled hard, and looked up at me. "Okay, that's the last one," he said. "Let's call the demon and get him here, so he can step into a circle of salt and you can have your body back."

"God, I hope this works," I said, as he dug his phone out of his pocket and scrolled through his recent calls until he found *Mal.*

He called my phone, which was presumably in the possession of the demon who'd stolen my body, putting it to his ear.

I tried to act casually, as if listening in on a conversation between my new boyfriend and my demon body-thief was no big deal.

"Going to voicemail," Henry told me, "so I'll leave a message."

I nodded. Good plan.

"Hey!" Henry said after my *You've reached Malcolm Goodman*

message played. "Malcolm! It's me, Henry. How are you? I haven't seen you since Halloween, but I wanted to let you know that the money finally came in. The twenty thousand dollars I owe you, from the Gorfney project?"

All of that was a brazen lie. He owed me no such thing, plus he'd seen—or heard—me daily since the party. But he said it *so* convincingly, I almost believed it myself.

"*And* I'm gonna stop you before you call me back," Henry continued, "because I know you're gonna ask me to wire it to you, but I'm sorry, this time I can't. I need your signature for the tax forms. And none of this electronic shit. You gotta come here and give me your old-fashioned John Hancock before I can release the check." He took a deep breath. "Okay, that's it. See you soon."

And with that, he hung up.

I waited a few extra seconds to make sure the connection was cut. And then I said, "That was brilliant. Who's *not* going to come pick up an easy twenty thousand dollars? All we have to do now is lure him into one of the hidden salt circles, break the orb, and... I'm free." I thought about what I'd just said and frowned. "That seems almost too easy."

Henry laughed—and I looked at him closely, because... I don't really know why. Maybe his laughter sounded a little... forced...?

He kissed me. "You need it to be harder?" he asked.

"No," I said, pulling him close. "I just... I feel like I'm missing something."

Henry kissed me again. "We're ready," he reassured me. "And... since we're in wait-mode, I'm gonna do a quick workout, just in the yard." He started to go, but then turned back, concern in his eyes. "Will you be okay?"

I nodded. Yeah. I knew he used running, in particular, as a form of stress-reduction. And since it had been a few days since he'd last gone for a run, I wasn't going to keep him from an in-the-yard workout on this enormously stressful day.

He left his phone near me on the coffee table—in case the demon called back. Not that I could answer it, but I could certainly let Henry know about the call. He smiled and kissed me again, then went into his bedroom to change.

Still, I found myself wondering...

"What aren't you telling me?" I murmured.

Henry's computer was on the coffee table, so I sat down in front of it, and opened the *Crimson Book.*

I was getting faster at typing, but it still took forever, so I tried to use the book's *recent history* to find the page that Henry had accessed about reclaiming a hostage-body from a demon. Weirdly, though, the search history had been completely cleared. Henry must've done that by accident.

I tried to remember the phrases Henry had searched for. It was something like... *Rescue hostage body from demon,* comma, *orb...*? I typed it in.

Jesus, there was a *lot* of information here. I scanned through it, reading quickly.

"Okay, this is new, to *me,* at least," I said. "If you say *In hac oscula, meus es tu,* you can force the demon to..." I leaned in closer to read the small print. "...*possess* you with a *kiss...*?" I thought about that for about half a nano-second. "Ew. *Why* would you want to do *that*?"

"Hey."

I looked up to see Henry in the doorway. He was dressed for his workout, and carrying the box that held the remainder of the salt. We'd used about half of it.

"I'm gonna put the rest of the salt in the garage," he told me. "Don't want Demon-Mal to see it, get spooked, and run."

Wow, yes, that was smart. "Good thinking," I agreed.

After giving me one more reassuring, *We got this* smile, Henry humped the box of salt toward the front of the house. I heard the door open as I turned my attention back to the computer and leaned in to read more.

There was a lot here about shattering the orb—it was important to break it into small pieces or the demon might survive. Duly noted.

I found info, too, about the orb as a vessel. The demon had been trapped—somehow—inside of it, which really must've sucked. As the spirit of a hostage-body, or so the *Crimson Book* said, my imprisonment was far more free-range.

But yes, as I'd discovered during Henry's last windy run, I had to remain in relatively close proximity to the orb, or—oh, shit. Straying too far from the orb—violating its rules—would apparently cause me to be absorbed into the vessel. The sensation of being absorbed, the *Book* reported, had been described by the rare survivors as if one were dissolving. The end result was that I'd be trapped in the orb as completely as the demon had been, which again would suck.

And that phrase *rare survivors* wasn't making me too happy either.

And, whoa, wait, *what* was this...?

"Here's more you didn't tell me," I muttered. *"Do not risk breaking the orb until the hostage-body is safely within the confines of the salt-circle. Doing so...* What...? *Doing so will allow the demon to* steal *the hostage-body's soul and take it back with him to the Beyond...?* Fuck, the *Beyond* sounds pretty awful..."

Henry's phone—which he'd left on the table—buzzed, startling me out of my reverie of what, exactly, the *Beyond* might be.

He was getting a text, and it wasn't from Gina.

It was from me.

It was weird to see his phone light up with my name. Weirder still to picture my phone being held in my hands—my body completely controlled by a demon—probably still somewhere in Las Vegas.

On my way. The text read. *How abt 6 pm. Will u b home?*

Jesus, Demon-Me texted like a teenager from 1995. Hmm. I wonder how long he'd been trapped in that orb....

I couldn't bring the phone to Henry, but I could deliver the message. Six o'clock—that was hours from now.

Henry'd left the front door open, and I went onto the porch.

He was nowhere in sight.

It was a lovely day—blue sky, sunshine, birds singing, bees buzzing. Henry's well-tended garden was an oasis of peacefulness and calm, and I took a deep breath.

But then Henry came charging around from the side of the house—hurtling and hurdling as he leapt over bushes and clumps of tall grass. He must not've seen me standing there—he was moving pretty fast—as he blew through his front yard and disappeared around the other side of the house, through the driveway's gate. "Whoa," I said. "That's a new exercise."

I didn't have to wait long for him to make a full circuit—his house just wasn't that big.

And when he appeared again, bursting out from around the corner, I said, "Hey!" and then bellowed *"Heeeyyy!!"*

He heard the hurricane-force winds and skidded to a stop. He knew immediately why I was out there. "Did the demon call back?"

"He texted," I reported. "He'll be here at six."

"Great!" Henry checked his watch as he nodded. "That's great! I'm almost done—once more around, then I'm gonna walk it a few times, mindfully, to lower my heart-rate. Won't take me too long..."

He seemed to want some sort of response from me, so I nodded. I was feeling guilty that he had to do this instead of going for a normal run.

But he didn't seem to mind. He nodded back cheerfully, then dashed away.

I went back inside, acutely aware that, since the demon was arriving at six, these could be my last few hours alive. Or at least this form of *alive* that I currently was, which was probably better than what I'd be if I got sucked to the Beyond with the demon.

I walked through Henry's house, memorizing it: his quirky, comfortable furniture, the art—including his incredible photographs—on the walls, the bedroom that, in very short order I'd come to think of as *ours*. I didn't want to leave here. I didn't want to leave *him*. For the first time in my life, I actually wanted to stay.

"Please let this work," I whispered.

Henry

"Please let this work." I exhaled the words on the release of my final meditative breath, as I ended my cool-down in the middle of my front yard.

I gave one final shake to each of my feet, pretending it was part of my ritual, in case Mal was still watching.

I was glistening and sticky with sweat, so I brushed off my legs, already knowing what I'd tell Malcolm if he asked—that I'd run through a series of spider webs, and spiders were not welcome inside my house.

But I went in and shut the door, and he was nowhere in sight. I found him back in the living room, sitting in front of my computer.

He glanced up as I approached—he was trying hard to hide his worry.

I was doing the same as I picked up my phone and read the demon's text.

"Six is fine, I'm home all day," I recited my reply for Mal's benefit as I typed the words. "See you then."

I sent the text, and it whooshed its way to the demon who'd stolen Mal's body. Now we'd wait. *I'm gonna shower and grab something to eat*, I was just about to tell Malcolm, when the doorbell rang.

Malcolm immediately leapt up and off the sofa. "It's him," he said.

It was only 3:30.

"It's probably just Paul," I reassured him, and yeah, the timing was right—school was out. When I'd called, asking him to pick up the salt, he'd mentioned that the wrapping paper I'd ordered last month, from Joey's pre-school fundraiser, would be coming in some time this week.

"It's not," Mal insisted. "It's *him*. I feel it."

I was pretty certain that I was going to open the door to Paul and several rolls of festive Sponge-Bob patterned wrapping paper, but I didn't want to disrespect Mal, so I said, "Okay, just... stay here."

"Why do I feel it?" he was saying. "I mean, I *know* it. That is so fucking weird..." Then he noticed that I was leaving the living room, and he started pointing and whispering, "The orb, the orb, take the orb!"

But I wasn't going to take the orb to the front door—if it *was* Paul, Joey might've come with him, and the last thing I needed was for the kid to jump into my arms and make me drop it before the demon returned Mal's body.

"Shit, Henry!" I heard Mal stage-whisper.

And *shit* was putting it mildly, because when I opened the door, it wasn't Paul and Joey standing there. Mal had been right. It was, indeed, the demon.

He looked like Mal, and yet, he somehow didn't. And it wasn't just that his hair and clothes were different. There was an edge to him—a tightness, a jagged and jarring brittleness—not just to his face but even in the way he stood.

He was a hard Mal, a mean Mal, a Mal without the real Mal's generous, open, loving heart.

He stepped through the screen and into the house like he owned the place, closing the door tightly behind him.

He gave me a smile that seemed to shimmer with micro-expressions of, well, evil. And maybe that was just me knowing he was a demon, but I don't think so. It was creepy as hell.

"My four o'clock cancelled," Demon-Malcolm said in a voice

that was Mal's and yet not Mal's, "and I was in your 'hood. Just got your text so I thought I'd drop by."

He was standing in the middle of the doormat—directly in the center of the salt circle that was hidden beneath it.

"Shit!" I said. I should've listened to Mal—real Mal's—instincts and grabbed the orb. If I had, I could've broken it right now, and this all would've been over, just like that. But the orb was back in the living room.

Demon-Malcolm raised an eyebrow. "Problem...?"

Yeah, I'd just inadvertently shouted *Shit* in his face. "No!" I said quickly. "I just, um..." Think, think... "Realized I still have to print out the tax forms for you to sign—I wasn't expecting you til later. But why don't you come on back, let me get that printed."

CHAPTER TWENTY
Malcolm

I was right. The demon who stole my body had arrived early.

We weren't ready.

Were we ready…?

I wasn't ready, but God, I hoped that Henry was…

It was weird as hell to be standing in the living room and yet hear myself chatting away with Henry in the entryway, as he let me into the house.

I backed into the corner, away from Henry's computer, trying to hide. I honestly didn't know if the demon would be able to see me, or if, like everyone who *wasn't* Henry, he'd have no idea that I was there in the room. I tried to blend in with a standing lamp as Henry somehow managed to keep up the small talk with that thieving demon fuck.

"So how've you been?" I heard Henry say. He sounded like his usual cheerful, low-key Henry-self. "Gina told me you went up to Vegas with some hot new guy. That's intriguing."

"Oh, yeah, no," I heard myself say, "that didn't end well."

Jesus, what did *that* mean? Had I merely broken up with the poor, unsuspecting cute guy from those photos, or had I killed him and eaten his brains? No, probably not the brain-eating—that was a zombie thing. My demon wasn't *that* kind of undead.

I hoped.

"Ah, sorry to hear that," Henry said.

As I lurked in the corner, Henry breezed into the room. He looked around for me, briefly meeting my eyes, but disguised it as pretending to look for his computer, which he scooped up and carried over to his printer station. He set it down and plugged in the USB.

But then there he came—strutting into the room. Demon-Me.

Sweet baby Jesus. I stared at him—at myself—transfixed.

The demon wore my body like an ill-fitting suit—and it certainly didn't help that he was wearing... an ill-fitting suit. Track suit, that is. It was blindingly bright blue, with white stripes down the legs. He'd definitely gotten trapped in the orb in the 1990s. The last of my doubts about that were erased.

I don't think I made a noise—I certainly kept any *Holy Fucking Goddamn Shit!* type exclamations inwardly aimed and silent. But Demon-Me suddenly turned and looked directly at Spirit-Me. And I'm talking dead in the eyes.

He saw me and held my gaze, as if not merely able to see me, but also capable of reading my mind.

And just like that, he turned to look directly at the red-glowing orb on Henry's bookshelf, and then down at the rug beneath his feet.

"There's no twenty grand is there?" He snarled, his voice guttural with anger. "Fuck!"

"Henry!" I shouted, "Smash the orb! Do it now!"

He'd been pretending to focus on his computer as he shifted his body closer to the orb, but now he looked up, startled.

But we were too late—Demon-Me jumped off the rug, and out of the salt circle.

"I can see your invisible friend," it told Henry. "In fact, now that we're... reunited, I know *everything* he's thinking. Salt circle under the rug? Not gonna happen."

If he knew about *this* salt circle, then he knew about the one in the kitchen, too, although I tried desperately not to think about it.

The demon seemed to grow larger, expanding with his rage as he pulled himself up to my full height. I was bigger than Henry. Broader. If I got violent, I could do some serious damage to him.

"Henry, watch out," I breathed, fearing the thing would attack him. Henry's getting physically hurt by the demon was a danger that I hadn't anticipated, but now that we were in the middle of this, it was all I could imagine. My stomach churned with fear and helplessness. In my current state, I could do little to defend him.

Not that I wasn't going to try...

But the demon just stood there and laughed, looking from Henry, to me, to the orb on the bookshelf, and back.

Where Henry was standing, he was closer to the orb, but the table was in his way. The demon, although farther from it, had a straight shot.

Breaking it while the demon wasn't standing in a salt-circle meant my soul was Beyond-bound. But if doing that meant saving

Henry's life...

I was more than ready and willing.

I was farthest from the orb out of all of us, but of course, I wasn't perceived as a threat. The demon clearly knew my limitations.

I inched closer to the orb as neither man moved. The demon stood there, ignoring me, his gaze locked with Henry's.

Whatever he saw in Henry's eyes made him take a deep breath and smile—but it was one fucking evil up-turn of my lips.

"I'm outa here," Demon-Mel said. "But just to be safe, I think I'll take the orb with me this time."

He moved then, but it was slowly. Casually. A saunter—taking care to step around the carpet and its hidden salt circle.

Henry and I both moved then, but Henry was faster and he beat me over to the shelf. He picked up the orb, holding it up over his head.

"Stay back," he warned the demon.

But Demon-Me kept coming, slowly moving closer. "Or what?" he asked in a voice that was oily and unpleasant. "You're gonna kill your boyfriend? Because that's what'll happen when the orb breaks. I'll be gone, but I *will* take him with me."

"Do it," I said. "Henry, do it. *Do it, do it, do it!*"

But Henry didn't move, and the demon just kept coming.

"Oh, look," he said. "Malcolm's willing to die for you. That's so romantic. But he can't break the orb himself. You've gotta do it."

"Stay! Back!" Henry said again.

"Henry, please," I begged, but he was so freaking calm and cool—he even smiled, just a little.

If that was meant to piss the demon off, it worked, because the thing growled, "This is getting boring. I think I'll just break your neck."

That was it for me. I lost it, rushing forward, screaming "*NOOOOOO!*" I was ready to tackle that motherfucker to the ground.

But before I could reach him, Henry's little smile got bigger as he told the demon, "I don't think so."

And he did it, thank God. He used both hands to throw the orb high into the air—up toward the room's vaulted ceiling on a trajectory that none of us could possibly intercept or catch.

I braced myself for its impending, shattering impact on the acid-washed concrete floor.

"Henry, I love you," I told him with what I assumed would be my last breath, but he'd turned toward the demon and caught him in a bear hug.

"*In hac oscula, meus es tu,*" Henry shouted, and I recognized those words—I'd read them in the *Crimson Book.*

But it wasn't until Henry kissed Demon-Mal, full on the mouth, that I realized exactly what those words were.

It was that stupid-ass spell, where you could force a demon to possess you with a kiss.

"Henry, don't!" I shouted. "The demon will possess *you!*"

But he did it so quickly—in those seemingly slow-mo seconds as the orb hung there in the air, before it smashed down onto the floor—and as I watched, the demon was expelled from my body and entered Henry's.

The force of the transfer pushed Henry's chest in as his shoulders came forward, and he released his grasp on me. He staggered backwards several steps, as with a whoosh and pop—it felt like hocking the world's largest and most disgusting loogie—I was suddenly back in my poorly dressed body.

The force of my repossession made me stagger backwards, away from Henry, too.

Which was a good thing, because the demon was now inside of Henry's body, and he was fucking pissed.

He snarled in anger and spat out the words, "You fucking idiot! You killed us both!"

He was talking to Henry, whose spirit was probably here, somewhere, but of course I couldn't see him. But he wouldn't be here for long—the demon was standing off of the rug, well outside of the salt circle, which meant he would take Henry with him to the Beyond.

"No!" I shouted as the orb hit the floor and shattered.

My heart shattered, too, into a million pieces.

Henry's hostage-body crumpled to the floor as the demon was sucked away.

"What did you do?" I cried as I rushed toward him, falling to my knees beside him and gathering him into my arms. "The demon was inside you, and you... No! No! Henry, please don't be dead!"

But Henry wasn't breathing—his body was limp, lifeless.

Dear God, he'd saved me, but he'd sacrificed himself to do it.

"Oh, Henry," I said. "No!"

I had to start CPR—first I had to fucking remember *how* to do it—and I was putting him flat onto the floor so I could start breathing for him, when he suddenly spasmed and then coughed.

Oh my God, he wasn't dead!

But he was coughing and choking—his entire body shuddering as he struggled to breathe. As I held him and tried to help him, I looked wildly around for his phone—to call 9-1-1.

But then his eyes opened.

"Henry!" I said. "How can I help?"

He clung to me. "Mal... Are you... back...?"

"Yes," I told him. "It's really me. I'm here."

He tried to sit up, but then turned away from me and vomited.

It was violent and hideous and incredibly noxious—thick and black and toxic—the remains of the demon, I assumed, as I held on to him tightly throughout the ordeal. These days his hair wasn't long enough to need holding back from his face, the way I'd done all those years ago when I'd first met Henry in the bathroom of the freshman dorm.

Our meet-cute, as Gina called it.

But now, just like then, I rubbed his shoulders and back and murmured soothingly, "Let it out... You're doing great... Just let it go..."

When he finally finished, he pulled off his shirt to use to wipe his face and mouth, telling me, "I'm okay."

I wanted to do nothing more than listen to him breathe and feel his heart beating in his chest, so I pulled him away from his puddle of awfulness, and we just lay there on the floor together, with our arms around each other.

But I kept replaying that last crazy scene with the demon and...

"How are you not dead?" I finally asked Henry, adding, "I mean, I'm really glad you're not, but... when the orb broke, you weren't standing in a salt circle."

I felt him laugh, and he turned his head to smile up at me. "But I was," he said.

I was already shaking my head, *no*. I'd seen very clearly where he'd been standing, and he had *not* been on the rug.

"I made one outside," Henry told me.

I stared at him.

He nodded. "A big one, around the entire house. During that

workout...? I put salt in my pockets."

Holy fuck... Henry had taken that box of salt out to the garage, telling me that he didn't want the demon to see it, but in truth...

He smiled at my amazement. "I thought I could sprinkle it in a circle as I ran, but I realized pretty quickly that wasn't good enough. But then you came outside..."

I'd told him that the demon had texted him. And Henry'd then told *me* that he was going to cool down with some mindful walking—which really meant...

"Your mindful cool-down was really mindful salt-circle-making," I realized. "And you couldn't tell me about it because..."

"The *Book* said that when the demon was near you, it would know everything that you knew."

I hadn't known that. But that was a good thing, because if I had, I would've been completely in my head about *every*thing. As it was, I hadn't thought twice about Henry's announcement about his cool-down. And because I hadn't thought twice about it, the demon hadn't thought about it at all.

And neither the demon nor I had realized that he was already inside of a salt circle, just by being inside of this house.

"I'm sorry," Henry said now. "After I was all in your face for not talking to me..."

"*Not* the same thing," I reassured him. I looked at this man in my arms—my best friend, my lover, my everything, and I realized exactly what he'd done. Yes, he'd made that salt circle around his house, but he'd refused to take a chance with my life. He'd first freed my body by making the demon possess him in that split second of time before the orb broke—and if the circle of salt he'd made hadn't worked, *he* would've spent eternity in the Beyond with the demon. "Not even close."

Henry's smile was like the sunrise. "By the way, it was sexy as hell that you were willing to die for me."

No shit—that went both ways. I leaned in to kiss him, but he pulled away.

"Oh my God, no! Demon vomit!" Henry covered his mouth with his hand.

I looked at him. "I don't care. I'm pretty sure the demon smoked. Demon vomit will be an improvement over ashtray mouth."

I kissed him—and he laughed.

"Jesus," Henry said. "You weren't kidding."

I laughed, too. No, I was not.

But Henry kissed me again, anyway.

And when I pulled back to smile into his eyes, I realized...

"The sun's going down," I told him. "Do you... want to watch the sunset?"

The look Henry gave me said *Really...?* And I laughed, because when did he ever *not* want to watch the sunset.

He was already on his feet, and held out his hand to help me up.

He followed me into his entryway where I opened his front door. Easily. Effortlessly. With full human strength.

We went outside, into Henry's gorgeous, peaceful garden and just stood there, our arms around each other, gazing up at the beauty of the evening sky.

"And so Ashtray Mouth and Vomit Breath," I couldn't resist whispering into Henry's ear, "lived happily ever after."

He laughed. "Yeah," he said, correctly interpreting my subtext. "I love you, too."

EPILOGUE
A Week Later
Henry

The binding spell had been broken when Malcolm's spirit returned to his body.

Which was not a problem.

But Mal was pretty adamant about the fact that the sex we'd had while under that binding spell was… well, I believe his words were: "Fucking epic."

After cleaning up demon vomit, vacuuming up orb shards, showering, and both brushing our teeth for about an hour, I texted Gina to let her know that everything was okay, and that Mal was back. I also left a message for Pat, canceling our Thursday at four AM.

Mal ordered both pizza and Chinese food as I baked him a *Welcome Home* cake.

After we ate, we crawled in bed.

And spent about a week there.

As far as I was concerned, the sex continued to be "fucking epic," even without the help of the binding spell. Mal insisted that the *I feel everything you feel* nature of the binding spell had given him a crash course in how to rock my world. But he also said that his memories of feeling everything that I'd felt were an incredible turn-on, and he wished that I'd had a chance to experience that, too.

I didn't care. I was just glad to have him back.

But on Saturday, I came inside after a run—a regular one, where I did my usual circuit of the neighborhood, this time *without* Mal tethered to me—to find him on my sofa in his underwear, his hair in full sexy bedhead mode, my laptop on his lap.

He'd still been in bed, fast asleep, when I'd gotten up.

"Good morning," I said, kissing him hello.

He smiled at me as he stood up, then clapped his hands three times as he spun in a circle, chanting, "*While the night is dark and the sun is bright I bring you a dance unto my sight.*"

Suddenly, I was stomping and spinning around the room.

"Oopsie," he said, standing there laughing at me. "That's the Irish Step Dancing spell. It must be the other one." He snapped his fingers. "That's right, there was salt..."

"Malcolm!" I shouted as I continued to stomp.

He quickly made a salt circle with a carton he had at the ready—and I knew that this was not as *Oopsie, it was an accident* as he was pretending. I was being punished for all those spells I'd cast—spells that had made him spit Morse Code and do mime and even make shadow animals on the wall.

Or maybe I wasn't being punished for casting the spells, but rather for laughing my ass off when he'd told me about them. I'd thought they hadn't worked, and yet he'd been... It still made me laugh to think about it. Even now. Especially now as I imagined him dancing around the room like this.

Mal laughed, too, as he stood in the middle of the circle and said, "*I bring you to my consciousness.*"

Just as it had before, a low-pitched noise started—a barely discernable hum.

"Mal, what are you doing?" I asked, still dancing as I tried to remember which spell he was casting now, and what was going to happen next.

He closed his eyes, his face tilted toward the ceiling, his arms outstretched. "*I bring you to me.*"

The humming sound intensified, and I was pulled—rather violently—into the circle. "Holy crap!" I shouted. He was casting the binding spell—and this time he was binding *me* to *him*. Apparently that *only do it once* thing really meant that we could do this twice—once per binder and bindee.

Mal raised his voice to be heard over the hum. "*I bind you to me as I bind myself to you!*"

There was a blast of light and it knocked both of us out of the salt circle and onto our asses as the humming sound crescendoed with a crash, then stopped.

A sudden wind came out of nowhere and blew the salt on the floor, breaking the circle.

I stared at Mal.

He grinned at me. "Smack me," he said.

"What?" I said. "No."

"Not hard," he said as he held out his hand. "Do it."

I gave him a low five—slightly harder than I otherwise might've and...

"Ow!" We both said it at the same time.

Mal was delighted as he got to his feet and pulled me up, too. "It worked! You feel what I feel." He started to tug me with him toward the hallway.

"Where are we going?"

"Where do you *think* we're going?" he countered, bee-lining it for our bedroom. "Since neither of us are spirits, the *Crimson Book* says this spell won't last long, maybe an hour, tops, so hurry. And speaking of tops, babe, you're on top."

As Mal caught my mouth with his, I realized what he'd done—and that I was now going to feel everything that *he* felt when we...

Of course, as soon as we kicked the bedroom door closed, my phone rang. "It's Gina," I said.

"What a surprise," Mal said as he took off my T-shirt.

"I'm putting it on silent," I announced.

"She'll understand," Mal said as he yanked down my shorts and pulled me with him onto the bed.

We looked at each other then, and we both laughed, and Mal added, "No, she won't. But that's okay."

"Do you think she'll *ever* believe us?" I wondered.

"Shhh," Mal said. "Stop talking and kiss me."

So I did.

FYI, Mal was right about the binding spell.

And, as he was fond of saying for the entire rest of our long and happy lives, "They lived fucking epically ever after."

Dear Reader,

The book you've just read might be one of my all time personal favorite stories.

And yeah, yeah, I know that authors generally tend to fall hopelessly in love with whichever book they're working on in the moment, but this one really is special, in part because we're making it into a movie.

It's a bit of a creative Mobius strip, because it's the novelization of the screenplay—that we've yet to film—that I wrote with the help of my actor/director/producer son, Jason.

Here's how it went down: Jason and I talked story, character, structure, and he wrote a very early, very first-drafty version of the screenplay. I sat in on a table read via Skype, and as I was listening to Jason and his amazing co-star Kevin Held bringing the characters of Henry and Mal to life, I suddenly knew *exactly* what their story *really* was, and how to tell it. So after the read, I called Jason and said, "Hey, may I do a rewrite of the script?"

Jason said, "Sure, Mom! Great!"

And I said, "Okay, but maybe I need to be more clear. I want to take a machete to your screenplay and chop it into tiny unrecognizable bits and then do a REWRITE. I want to change this story radically, and instead of it being a romantic COMEDY, as you've written it, it will now be a ROMANTIC comedy. Is that okay?"

Jason laughed. And essentially said, "Go wild, go big, machete-chop away!"

So I outlined and I plotted and I used 3x5 cards with scene notes, and figured out how to wrestle Final Draft (a screenwriting program) to the ground, and in the course of about ten days, I wrote *that* version of this story in a screenplay format.

And I wrote it with Jason's and Kevin's voices as Henry and Malcolm loud and clear in my head.

So yeah. It was *really* fun to write.

Then, after we did yet *another* table read, and tweaked and revised and edited (because you know me, I always write long, and this movie could not be three hours), I realized, "Hey, you know what would be *really* fun? To write the romance novel version of this story, with two very strong first person point-of-view voices."

And so I did.

Even though this is a "novelization" of a screenplay, *every* book I've *ever* written has been the novelization of the movie that's playing in my head. It's just that *this* one is way, *way* more clear!

I also can tell you that, when I wrote the screenplay, I was writing the *romance novel* that I saw so very clearly in my head.

And what makes *this* particular project even more wildly fun, is that yes, those are our two stars, Kevin and Jason, on the cover.

Also…? We're going to be making an audiobook edition, and Kevin's going to read Mal's scenes, and Jason's gonna read Henry's. So if you love this story even half as much as I do, you can love it in ebook, print, audio, *and* get to watch the movie, too!

We're filming it in September 2018, out in California, with hopes of it being ready to watch in early 2019.

Check out our Kickstarter campaign, coming in summer 2018. Help crowd-fund the movie version of this book and get unique backer rewards!

Also: Be sure to check out our recently completed rom-com movie, *Analysis Paralysis*. I produced. It was written and directed by and stars my amazing son, Jason T. Gaffney and the deliciously funny and sexy Kevin Held. (It's funny AF. I've watched it 2,748 times in post, and I *still* laugh! Coming soon to you via LGBTQ film fests and then on to distribution…)

Back to regular "Dear Reader" letter stuff: If you enjoyed *Out of Body*, I'd appreciate it ginormously if you'd post a review or toss it some shiny stars and/or digital buckets o' love at your favorite on-line bookseller. You might've noticed that I've become an indie author, and I'm my own publisher now. (Ah, the freedom! OMG, the typos are now all mine!)

But authors, particularly indie authors, depend on reader reviews more than ever in this crazy, noisy, option-filled digital world. I'm very grateful, too, when you post, share, tweet, text, and talk about my books, particularly new ones like *Out of Body*. (Thank you so very, very much.)

Last but way not least, thank you for choosing to spend your precious reading time with my characters and me. Life is crazy these days (Summer 2018), with daily stressors that are enormous! (Please register and #VoteBlue!)

I love getting interactive: Twitter's my social media format of choice—give me a shout @SuzBrockmann. And if you want to be absolutely certain you'll get hot-off-the-press news about upcoming new releases (like oh, say, my next TDD book, featuring Thomas and Tasha), reissues, appearances, and e-book deals, go to:
www.suzannebrockmann.com/about/news-from-suz
to sign up for my enewsletter!

Love and hugs and NEVER stop fighting for equality, hope, peace, and love,

Suzanne Brockmann

More from Suzanne Brockmann:

Troubleshooters Series
1. *The Unsung Hero*
2. *The Defiant Hero*
3. *Over the Edge*
4. *Out of Control*
5. *Into the Night*
6. *Gone Too Far*
7. *Flashpoint*
8. *Hot Target*
9. *Breaking Point*
10. *Into the Storm*
11. *Force of Nature*
12. *All Through the Night*
13. *Into the Fire*
14. *Dark of Night*
15. *Hot Pursuit*
16. *Breaking the Rules*
17. *Headed for Trouble* (anthology)
18. *Do or Die*
19. *Some Kind of Hero*

Troubleshooters Short Stories and Novellas
1. *When Tony Met Adam*
2. *Beginnings and Ends*
   (A Jules & Robin Short Story)
3. *Free Fall*
4. *Home Fire Inferno*
5. *Ready to Roll*
6. *Murphy's Law*

Tall, Dark & Dangerous Series
1. *Prince Joe*
2. *Forever Blue*
3. *Frisco's Kid*
4. *Everyday, Average Jones*
5. *Harvard's Education*
6. *Hawken's Heart*
   (It Came Upon a Midnight Clear)
7. *The Admiral's Bride*
8. *Identity: Unknown*
9. *Get Lucky*
10. *Taylor's Temptation*
11. *Night Watch (Wild, Wild Wes)*
12. *SEAL Camp*
13. *Thomas King's Princess*
    (coming soon)

Fighting Destiny Paranormal Series
0.5 *Shane's Last Stand* (e-short prequel)
1. *Born to Darkness*

Night Sky YA Series
(with Melanie Brockmann)
0.5 *Dangerous Destiny*
   (e-short prequel)
1. *Night Sky*
2. *Wild Sky*

Stand-Alone Romance
Out of Body (New 2018)
HeartThrob
Body Language
Embraced by Love
Future Perfect
Give Me Liberty
Ladies' Man
Stand-in Groom
Letters to Kelly
Scenes of Passion
Undercover Princess (Rita Award Winner)

Sunrise Key Series
1. *Kiss and Tell*
2. *The Kissing Game*
3. *Otherwise Engaged*

Stand-Alone Romantic Suspense
Body Guard (Rita Award winner)
Infamous
Time Enough For Love
Hero Under Cover
Love With the Proper Stranger
No Ordinary Man

Bartlett Brothers Series
1. *Forbidden*
2. *Freedom's Price*

St. Simone Series
1. *Not Without Risk*
2. *A Man to Die For*

ABOUT THE AUTHOR

After childhood plans to become the captain of a starship didn't pan out, **Suzanne Brockmann** took her fascination with military history, her respect for the men and women who serve, her reverence for diversity, and her love of storytelling, and explored brave new worlds as a *New York Times* bestselling romance author. Over the past twenty-five years she has written fifty-seven novels, including her award-winning Troubleshooters series about Navy SEAL heroes and the women—and sometimes men—who win their hearts. In addition to writing books, Suzanne Brockmann produces feature-length movies: the award-winning romantic comedy *The Perfect Wedding*, which she co-wrote with her husband, Ed Gaffney, and their son, Jason; the thriller *Russian Doll*; and the soon-to-be-released rom-com *Analysis Paralysis*. She is currently in pre-production for *Out of Body*, a rom-com with paranormal elements. She has also co-written two YA novels with her daughter Melanie, and is the publisher and editor of an m/m line of category romances called *Suzanne Brockmann Presents*. In 2018, Suz was given the Nora Roberts Lifetime Achievement Award from the Romance Writers of America. Her latest novel is *SEAL Camp*, available in print and e-book from Suzanne Brockmann Books, and in audio from Blackstone Audio.

Website: www.SuzanneBrockmann.com
e-Newsletter: www.tinyletter.com/SuzanneBrockmann
Twitter: @SuzBrockmann
Bookbub: www.BookBub.com/authors/suzanne-brockmann
Facebook: www.Facebook.com/SuzanneBrockmannBooks

Made in the USA
Monee, IL
13 February 2020